Seaforth Prison

The Haunted Series

Book 3

Patrick Logan

Books by Patrick Logan

The Haunted Series

Book 1: Shallow Graves
Book 2: The Seventh Ward
Book 3: Seaforth Prison
Book 4: Scarsdale Crematorium

Insatiable Series

Book 1: Skin
Book 2: Crackers
Book 3: Flesh
Book 4: Parasite
Book 5: Stitches

Family Values Trilogy

Witch (Prequel)
Mother
Father
Daughter

Short Stories

System Update

PROLOGUE

WARDEN BEN TRISTEN RUBBED his eyes and leaned back in his chair. The old metal creaked, an annoying grating sound, but one that he was familiar with, having sat in it nearly every day for the past eighteen years. There was a time when the sound had bothered him, and he had even considered replacing it at his own cost, but he had decided against it.

And now he was glad he had.

The chair was like an accomplice, an old partner that offered him predictable comfort in his ever-changing environment.

It was mid-evening, around the time that the twenty-two inmates should have been wrapping up their meals. That was another thing that he had initially loathed, but which now offered him solace: the rigid schedule and structure of Seaforth Prison. Inmates ate at the same time every day—*every day*, it didn't matter if it was Christmas, New Year's, their birthdays. Always the same time.

Ben's eyes drifted to the pictures on his desk, his gaze eventually falling on a picture of his best friend in the entire world. He loved his dog, a Boxer named Easton, for many of the same reasons he loved the mealtimes and his chair: Easton was predictable, reliable. His eyes drifted to the other photograph on his desk. His ex-wife and daughter? Less so.

With a heavy sigh, Ben rubbed his massive hands together, trying to work out the knots that had formed in the joints over the past several years. The doc said this stiffness was normal, a natural part of aging, but Ben never thought himself a normal man. At six foot three and two hundred and thirty-five pounds of solid muscle, Ben Tristen was hardly a normal seventy-two-year-old man. So he loathed when the doctor referred to anything that happened to him as 'normal', the way he now loathed any hiccup in Seaforth's schedule.

Ben prided himself in keeping in shape, and not in the way that other people his age exercised, which usually consisted of going to the gym three times a week to walk on a treadmill and do some awkward curls followed by bench pressing a stack of paper. No, Ben was different. He preferred the power movements, clean, squat, bench.

The basics for building muscle and strength, both of which came in handy as the warden.

As Ben started to daydream about his next workout, the phone on his desk suddenly rang, snapping him out of his own head. A frown formed on his heavily lined face.

The phone rarely rang in Seaforth.

This was not part of the routine.

He snatched it up before it could ring a second time.

"Warden here."

"Ben? Ben, you there?" The frantic nature of the man's voice on the other end of the line made Ben sit up straight in his chair, the old chair squealing in protest.

"Lenny? What's going on?"

There was shouting on the other end of the line, and Ben started to rise.

"Lenny! Answer me!"

The warden's sore fingers instinctively went to the wooden cross that hung around his neck and they started to massage it.

"Ben, it's Carson," Lenny finally replied. "You need to get here—you need to get here quick."

Carson.

Just the simple mention of the man's name was enough to get Ben to hang up the phone and run from the room.

***

In Seaforth, running was only permitted in the yard. Even the guards and Ben himself were forbidden from doing it.

But this was an exception.

It was an exception because of Carson.

Just the mention of Seaforth's most violent, sadistic, and infamous of prisoners was enough for Ben to break his own rule.

Only after checking that both the pistol and his Taser, which he rarely wore nowadays, were affixed to his hip.

Carson was held in Cell Block E, the only inmate currently in that block. It had been more than a year since Carson was held with the general population. A month before his move, Carson had strangled two gangbangers who'd thought they were tough, with inclinations of making a quick name for themselves by taking out the most infamous man at Seaforth.

They had found out the hard way that Carson was best left alone—with him, there were never any second chances.

Their multiple life sentences turned out to be rather short.

And if there were no inmates in Cell Block E, then that meant that…

Ben picked up the pace, tearing down the main corridor, ignoring the jeers and shouts from the prisoners locked in their cells flanking either side of him.

At the end of the hallway there was a single door, one that he promptly reached. But before he could knock, it was yanked open, and one of the more junior guards, a wiry black man named Perry, opened it, his eyes wide, bulging.

"Warden, you—"

Ben almost slapped him.

"Don't open the door!" he shouted. "You don't *just* open the door! How many times do I have to tell you? Use the camera! Check with Peter upstairs! Fuck, Perry!"

The man dropped his gaze.

"I'm sorry, it's just—"

"Look at me!" Ben ordered as he stepped over the threshold. Perry's eyes immediately shot up. Ben extended a finger, which looked a little more gnarled than usual, at the man's navy uniform. "Never *just* open the door. Not for me, not for nobody. Radio Peter, get him to check the cameras first. You got that?"

The man nodded quickly and Ben pushed past him.

"Fuck," Ben grumbled. "Nearly three million dollars on fancy cameras and security, and nobody even wants to use the damn thing."

Ben fondled the keycard affixed to his belt.

"Where's Quinn? He down there with Carson?"

Perry swallowed hard and again nodded as Ben strode into the whitewashed holding area that led to two other doors. The one on the right led to the yard, while the left led to the inmates' mess hall.

On the other side of the mess hall was the door that led to Cell Block E. Ben scanned his keycard and entered the mess hall.

Perry started to follow, but he held up a hand and stopped him, turning an ear to the inmates that were still shouting behind him.

"Keep them calm. No matter what, don't get them even more riled up. Calm. Got that?"

Perry nodded and then the door closed, shutting out both the sound and the man's frightened expression.

Ben hurried across the cement mess hall, his eyes fixed on the door at the other side. Heart racing, he reached for his keycard again, but before he could grab it, the door burst open and Deputy Quinn Laughlin stumbled through, his hands covering his face. Ben let out a sigh of relief.

His worst fear hadn't been realized.

Not yet, anyway.

"Quinn! What the fuck's going on? What's going on with Carson?"

The man said nothing; instead, he continued to stumble forward, his hands cupping his eyes.

"Quinn! Quinn?"

Ben reached for the man, but the deputy turned away at the last moment.

"Go!" Quinn bellowed. "Go to Carson! Now!"

Confused, Ben took a small step backward.

What the fuck's going on?

"Quinn!"

"Just go!"

A shout from behind the man drove Ben through the still open door, leaving Quinn to tend to whatever wound or spit or feces-throwing incident that Carson had inflicted on him.

"I'll be back," Ben said over his shoulder as he entered Cell Block E.

Unlike the well-lit and sterile cells in the general population, Cell Block E was dank, the air filled with a briny smell as a result of the south wall being closest to the sea. Also unlike the gen pop, the four cells in Cell Block E didn't have bars. Instead, they had thick, wooden doors with a simple mail-slot style hole in the center to deliver food.

Carson was in the last cell; Ben knew this, because he had put him there himself. But even if he hadn't known, the two guards standing outside the door would have tipped him off.

Ben started running again. As he rushed toward them, the guard at the door closed the metal shutter on the delivery slot and then bent at the waist and started to vomit.

Only then did Ben see the body of a third guard lying still on the ground in the center of the hallway.

"*Hey*! What the fuck's going on?" Ben demanded for what felt like the fiftieth time.

The man who had been vomiting looked up at him with bloodshot eyes and wiped his mouth with the back of his hand.

Ben was within a dozen feet of them now, and he could see that there was a small pool of blood on the floor around the fallen guard.

"I'm sorry, Warden," the man said. Then he bent over and puked again.

"What the *fuck* happened?"

It was Lenny, a tall, thick man with sunken eyes—the one who had called him down here—who answered now.

"I don't know...we heard shouting, came running, but by then it was too late."

Too late?

Ben shoved the first guard aside and dropped to one knee beside the man on the ground.

"Fuck," he said, looking away. A quick breath to calm himself, and he turned back to the body.

The guard was on his back, hands at his sides. The blood wasn't from a neck wound as he might have expected, given that Carson had first gained notoriety for ruthlessly slitting the throats of at least thirteen people, but from his eyes.

The man's eyes were dark pits filled with semi-coagulated blood that quivered like undercooked eggs.

The rest of his face was covered in red streaks.

"Jesus," Ben muttered. Then his instincts took over. He dropped his ear to the man's chest, listening for the thump of his heart or the wheeze of a breath.

He heard neither.

Ben sat up and interlaced his sore fingers, prepping himself for chest compressions.

"Where the fuck is medical? Did you send for medical? And what are you guys just standing around for? Help me!"

He felt a hand on his shoulder, and his head whipped around.

"We tried, Warden—we did everything we could, but by the time we got here, it was already too late. I'm sorry, I know—" Lenny's voice faltered. "I know you and Quinn were close."

Ben recoiled at the mention of his friend's name, an image of his friend in the mess hall covering his face coming back to him.

"Quinn? What are you talking about? I just saw him...saw him with his hands—"

His eyes darted from Lenny's stern face to the man on the floor, his eyes scanning his uniform.

The tag on his chest read: Quinn Laughlin.

"No," Ben said softly. "It's a trick, I just...I just..."

He felt the hand on his shoulder again, but he shrugged it off.

"It's Quinn; Carson got to him. Don't know how, but—"

"No!" Ben suddenly bellowed, trying and failing to comprehend what was going on.

I just fucking saw him! How—?

Heart racing in his chest, he wiped some of the blood off the fallen man's cheeks.

"No," he moaned.

It *was* Quinn. He had no idea how, but it definitely was Quinn.

Ben shot to his feet so quickly that a bout of dizziness struck him.

"Ben? You—"

The warden shoved Lenny out of the way and braced himself against the thick wooden door of Carson's cell.

His breathing was coming fast and furious now, and he could feel his muscles getting tight.

With a flick of his wrist, he pushed the metal slider open and stared into Carson's cell.

The man was naked and sitting with his back to the door, revealing a network of scars, some old, some new. His shaved head glistened under the single bulb high above.

"Carson, what have you done?" he demanded. When the man didn't react, he raised his voice. "Carson!"

Carson slowly rose to his feet, moving from a seated position to standing without using his hands. Then he started to turn, his hands out in front of him.

"Welcome, Ben."

Carson was smiling.

"I'm sorry about your friend Quinn, Ben, I really am. But I needed him to see."

Ben's gaze dropped to the man's flattened palms, a single object laying on each.

His stomach lurched and he nearly succumbed to the urge to vomit.

On each of Carson's hands was one of Quinn's eyeballs, both pointed directly at Ben.

"I needed him to *see!*" Carson suddenly roared as he raced toward the door. "The Goat will *see!* He's coming, and when he gets here, he will *see!*" Then he started to laugh. "Daddy's finally coming home! Can't you feel it, Ben? Can't you feel it?"

Ben let the metal slide fall with a clank and then stepped away from the door, sweat breaking out all over his body.

Carson's shouts from inside were muffled through the thick wood, but his words were clear enough.

"Can't you feel it in your chest, Ben? A tightness? That's how you know, Ben…that's how you know he's close…the Goat is coming…he's coming home."

Ben closed his eyes and concentrated on blocking out the madman's ramblings.

How is this possible? How the fuck *did this happen?*

His hand instinctively went to the cross that hung around his neck and he squeezed it tightly.

Eyes still closed, he said, "Call Father Callahan."

Then he dropped to his knees and hugged his friend's corpse. "Please, get Father Callahan here as soon as you can."

And then, for the first time in nearly two decades — the first time since his wife had scooped up his only daughter and had left without so much as a note — Warden Ben Tristen started to cry.

Part I - Stormy Days, Stormy Nights

Chapter 1

ALLAN KNOX STOOD ON the front door of the cracked cement steps and gazed upward at the massive wooden door in wonderment. His heart was racing, his brow sweaty. His backpack, the same one he had been lugging around for years, suddenly felt way too heavy, the straps biting through his coat, which was too light for the frigid air, and pinched his shoulders.

I should go. I should just turn around and walk away. They don't need me.

He swallowed hard, trying to figure out what his next course of action should be.

Maybe they won't even be home.

Allan leaned backward and looked to the many leaden windows that lined the front of the Estate. Lights were on in several of them.

There goes that theory.

Allan hooked his thumbs between the straps of his backpack and his jacket, easing the pressure.

Maybe this is the wrong house.

But a quick glance around confirmed that it was indeed the correct house. The description of the cherub with the X'd out eyes in the fountain was spot on. Even though someone had tried to wash the X's away, he could still see their faint outline on the oxidized brass or stone or whatever the hell it was made of. And it wasn't just the statue; there were other things about the place that Robert Watts had posted online that were accurate.

The wrought iron gates that he had pushed through, for instance. The long, winding drive, the cracked exterior bricks of the Estate.

The gigantic goddamn wooden door that looked like it should be used as a drawbridge to cross a moat.

I should go.

And then, as if nodding would confirm this as his final decision, Allan took a step backward, and then another. A moment before turning and leaving, however, he heard the sound of a latch sliding from inside the estate. Allan was so surprised by the sound that he stumbled backward. A split second later, he lost his footing completely, landing hard on his ass. He cried out, and then grimaced at the sound of metal scraping on metal from inside his backpack.

The door opened and he found himself staring up at a pretty woman with short blonde hair. She was eying him suspiciously, her bright green eyes barely visible from beneath her furrowed brow.

"Who the fuck are you?" she demanded.

Allan swallowed hard, still wincing from the pain that radiated up from his tail-bone.

"R-r-r-obert," he stammered.

The woman pushed her lips together, making a duck face. He also thought she pushed her substantial chest out a little, but he couldn't be sure given the thick coat she was wearing.

"Your name is Robert? Is that it?"

Allan shook his head slowly.

"N-n-no, but—"

She pointed to her bust.

"You're saying I'm Robert? Do *I* look like a fucking Robert?"

"N-no, of course not, but—"

She waved him off, then leaned back into the house.

"Hey, Robert, get your ass down here, there's a little kid here to see you."

Allan frowned and pushed himself to his feet.

"My name's Allan," he said, extending his hand to the woman who remained in the doorway, hands crossed over her chest now.

She looked at his hand, but made no move to shake it.

"So you *can* speak. That makes you better than most of Robert's visitors."

There was some commotion inside the house, and then a man with brown hair and narrow features appeared behind the pretty woman.

"Yeah? What do you want?" he asked, and Allan couldn't help but smile. It was Robert Watts, exactly as he had pictured him after he had first found his posts online less than a year ago.

Ever since his parents had died more than ten years ago, Allan had wanted to be a ghost hunter. His passion had only intensified when he had seen his parents' spirits at the crash site. Since that time, Allan had spent nearly every waking hour reading every book he could get his hands on, visiting supposedly haunted houses, and interviewing so-called ghost hunters, but it was all bullshit.

That is, until he read about *Inter vivos et mortuos*, about the book *Between the living and the dead*—until he found out about Robert Watts, of course. And before he started to see the dead everywhere.

Allan's entire face lit up with a grin that he couldn't even come close to containing.

"Robert, my name's Allan, and I want to join your team."

Robert didn't react as he had hoped; instead of smiling, the man grimaced. The woman, on the other hand, remained stoic.

"Team? What the hell are you talking about?"

Allan slipped the bag off his shoulder and set about opening it.

"I want to join your team—I want to hunt ghosts like you, Robert."

Chapter 2

"WATCH THE VIDEO, TELL me what you see."

Father Callahan rubbed his eyes with an arthritic hand, but made no move to lean closer to the monitor. In fact, he didn't even look at it.

"I'm tired, Ben. Really tired. If it hadn't been you who called me, I would've never left my parish. It's been a long, long trip, and these old bones don't travel well anymore. And my eyes don't work so well anymore. Why don't you tell me what happened?"

The warden observed the man in the black robe, the wooden cross, one nearly identical to his own, hanging nearly to his navel given his stooped posture. Father Callahan was old, very old, and the man was right; he wasn't fit for travel, not anymore. But what choice did he have? Who else could he call? Who else would believe that his best guard, his best friend, had had his eyes gouged out by a psychopath, and yet he had seen Quinn more than a hundred yards from where his dead body lay?

Ben cleared his throat, massaged his sore hands, and then took a deep breath.

"I know, Father, I know. But before I tell you what happened, I need you to watch the video. I need you to tell me what you see. Please. I'm old, you're old, neither of us have time for games anymore—and this isn't one, Father. I'm—" His voice hitched, and he was forced to clear his throat to avoid it cracking completely. "I'm desperate here."

Father Callahan sighed, but he put his reading glasses on the end of his nose, and then tilted his head backward to look through them and at the oversized monitor.

"Thank you, Father," Ben said, before his voice transitioned to professional. "This is surveillance video from yesterday. Please, watch carefully."

Ben leaned over and pressed play, and the video started to roll.

Shot from above and from the left, the camera showed the last third of the hallway of Cell Block E, and was focused on Carson's cell door, which was firmly closed. The timestamp in the bottom left of the screen read: 5:55. Thirty seconds later, a man stepped into the scene, traveling down the hallway, a tray held in front of him.

"That's Quinn. He's going to drop the food off, as he does every day, at 5:55. Exactly 5:55, every day."

Father Callahan said nothing. He leaned in closer.

On screen, Quinn walked up to the door, knocked once, then opened the metal slide and put the tray on it.

"He's supposed to wait—"

Callahan hushed him, and Ben clamped his jaw shut. The man moved even closer to the monitor, his frizzy gray hair now blocking nearly all of Ben's view of the screen. It didn't matter; the warden had watched the video dozens of times already.

And he still didn't understand why Quinn did what he did. Which was why he had brought Father Callahan in—that and what had happened in the mess hall minutes afterward.

The two went back a long time, and if there was any man that Ben thought might have insight into something like this, it was Father Callahan.

Rumor had it that the man had seen some things...some things in a swamp that were similarly unusual, unexplainable.

Ben fingered his cross again.

The Goat will see! Daddy's coming home.

He shuddered.

On the video, the tray disappeared into the slot; then, as usual, Quinn reached out to slide the metal closed again. But when it was halfway down, he hesitated, moving his head closer to the slot as if Carson was saying something to him.

"No sound," he offered, but Callahan waved his hand, indicating for him to keep his mouth shut.

Ben obliged.

It was at this point in the video that things changed. After hearing whatever Carson had said, Quinn's face suddenly darkened, and then he did the inexplicable. His lips moved, then he reached down to his belt and flipped through the keys on the loop almost robotically. He found the key he was looking for, then slid it into the lock. Then Quinn opened the cell door and stepped inside.

That was when static filled the screen.

Father Callahan suddenly leaned back.

"What happened?" he asked in a hoarse voice.

Ben shrugged.

"Don't know exactly. There was some sort of power surge, lights flickered. Our IT guy is working on it. Power company said there was nothing on their end, but it happens every once in a while." He reached for the keyboard and started to fast-forward.

"There's no image for exactly three minutes, then" —he pressed play, fighting back tears now — "this."

The static suddenly vanished, revealing the exact same scene as before it had come, with the door partly open, the hallway empty. And then Quinn stumbled out, his hands covering his eyes, blood spilling from between his fingers. His shoulder bumped the door, throwing it wide, and then he fell to one knee. A second later, he collapsed on his face, unmoving, where he lay until the other officers arrived. But just before Lenny and Paul came and flipped him over, a shadowy figure could be seen just inside the doorway. And then Carson reached out and slowly shut his cell door.

A few minutes after that, Ben himself appeared in the shot. The warden shut off the tape.

"I don't understand..." Ben said softly, more to himself than the priest. "I mean, what would make Quinn go in there?"

Father Callahan was still frozen, his eyes locked on the now black screen.

"And why didn't Carson leave? He had a perfect opportunity to leave, but he didn't. Instead, he actually *closed* the cell door. Why would he do that, Father?"

Ben cracked his knuckles, the gnarled joints creaking instead of popping in protest. Then he ground his teeth and flexed the muscles in his arms and chest.

"What the fuck would possess him to do that?"

Father Callahan finally leaned back from the screen.

"As you know, Ben, my eyes don't work as well as they used to. In fact, they barely work at all. But I think I saw the guard's lips move before he went into the cell. Did you catch that?"

"Uh-huh. Like I said, no sound...I tried slowing it down, zooming in and all that. Still can't figure it out. Looks like 'toast', maybe. 'Ghost'? 'Oat'? No fucking clue."

Father Callahan suddenly recoiled like he had been struck in the chest. The man stumbled backward, and Ben shot to his feet and grabbed the elderly priest before he toppled.

"Callahan, you alright?"

The man reached up and gripped Ben's shoulders, breathing deeply.

"N-n-no," he stammered. "Not oat, but *Goat*. And the reason why the man didn't leave is because he's waiting for someone to come and get him."

Ben felt a chill race up his spine.

The Goat will see…Daddy's coming home.

Chapter 3

"LET ME GET THIS straight, you read about me...about us...on the Internet? You think we are some sort of—what—modern-day ghostbusters?"

Six months had passed since purging the Seventh Ward, but to Robert Watts, it still felt like it had only been yesterday. And his limp was a perpetual reminder of his time there.

The kid on the couch across from him looked down.

"I didn't—I mean, I didn't mean to offend you or anything—"

"How, exactly, did you find out about me?" Robert asked sharply.

Allan looked up.

"You weren't that hard to find, not really. I mean, I didn't exactly know what I was looking for at first, but I always cruise the sites—the hidden ones, like where I found you—asking specific questions, trying to find anything about the Marrow, about quiddity, about spirits trapped on this side. That's how I found you."

Cal's beer overflowed and foam splashed to the floor following mention of *Marrow* and *quiddity*. Robert shot him a look, and then his eyes darted over to Shelly. She was standing behind the man—*kid, he's just a kid*—her arms crossed over her chest, her lips pressed together tightly.

Typical Shelly pose.

"What do you know about the Marrow?" Robert asked accusingly.

The boy's gaze fell again.

"Look, I'm sorry—I'll leave if you want. I'm not wanting for trouble. I just thought—I mean, when my parents died all those years ago, I saw them…I mean, I saw them even *after* their bodies were gone. And that sent me on this path. I want to know about them, about where they are, how they are, *who* they are. I found some stuff on the 'net, but not much. Nothing more than what you guys have probably read, about the sand, the water, the quiddity. And then there is the book; I kept hearing about this book, *Inter vivos et mortuos*. I almost gave up, too, but recently I've seen more—"

"Wait, you *saw* your parents? You see quiddity?" Cal interrupted.

Allan nodded.

"Sometimes with just my eyes, but not always—hold on a sec." The boy reached down and started to unzip his backpack.

Shelly unfolded her arms from her chest.

"No, you hold on a sec," she said, taking a large step forward. Allan craned his neck up to look at her, his eyebrows raised.

She held out a hand.

"Let me see your bag first."

The boy made a face and Robert leaned back.

"Calm down, Shelly. He's just a boy, he's—"

She squinted at him.

"Yeah, let's be safe, all right?" She hooked a chin to the three parallel scars that ran from Cal's cheek to his top lip. "Remember what happened last time when we were taken by surprise? Remember—"

Robert waved an arm.

He wasn't in the mood to head down memory lane.

"All right, fine. Check the bag."

Allan nodded at him as if he'd been waiting for Robert's permission before handing it over.

Shelly made a face as she rummaged through the myriad of cameras and other foreign-looking equipment. Allan cringed at the sound of scraping metal, but she eventually shrugged and handed it back.

"Just a bunch of voyeur shit—Cal, you probably have the same in your room to peek on me in the shower."

Cal didn't smile.

"Very funny."

"Guys, let him talk," Robert implored. Then to Allan, he said, "You were saying about with your eyes or...?"

The fear and anxiety that had been on the boy's face since he arrived—nerves, probably, although the idea that it was from meeting Robert made him uncomfortable—suddenly washed away.

"Yeah, I see them sometimes with my eyes, but what I found is that with this"—he pulled a regular-looking DSLR camera from his bag and fiddled with the lens—"I can see more." He raised an eyebrow. "A *lot* more."

Cal made a face.

"There are more of them?"

Allan smiled, which made him look even younger than his eighteen or so years.

"Oh yeah, *so* many more—but that's only recently. For years, I would only pick up one or, if I was lucky, two a month, trolling around a cemetery or around an accident. But recently..." He took a deep breath. "Recently they're *everywhere*. You know what I think?"

No one answered, but Allan continued anyway, pushing his round spectacles up the bridge of his small nose.

"I think something's happening. Something's changing."

Robert swallowed hard, Sean Sommers's last comments repeating in his mind.

The man warned never to go back, that the divide between this world and theirs—Leland Black's fiery world—was growing thinner each and every day.

He's your father.

He shook his head. Leland wasn't his father; Sean was off his fucking rocker with that one.

"How do we know you're not just a fake? A hack reporter or something, a Nigerian prince that wants our credit cards?" Shelly asked, her voice stern.

Allan stared directly at Robert when he spoke.

"Because," he said, fiddling with the lens on the end of the camera. He flicked a switch and a red light popped on. "I can show you."

Chapter 4

"YOU ARE A MAN of faith, Ben, I know this," Father Callahan said, his voice cracking. "Even though you left my parish years ago, I can tell by the way you fiddle with your cross—the one I gave you—that you are a good student of God."

Ben nodded as the crooked man spoke. They had since turned off the monitors and were now sitting in the staff room across from each other.

"Yes, I believe, Father. Ever since…well, for a long while now I have tried to stay true." He looked around at the plain white walls, the plastic tables; even in the staff room, the tables were made of thin plastic, just in case the inmates managed to get in here. "Especially in this place."

Father Callahan nodded, and for a minute or so neither man said anything. The silence made Ben uncomfortable, which was strange given that he was often alone with his thoughts.

And he usually liked it.

Now, however, his mind was filled with horrible images of his friend, hands clasped to his face, and of Carson, holding the eyes in his palms, a lecherous grin on his face.

The Goat…

But Ben didn't interrupt Father Callahan's train of thought. The man wasn't one of the rambling priests that he often caught on TV, spewing whatever religious clichés that came to mind. Rather, Callahan was a man who chose his words wisely. And it appeared as if this time, given what had happened, that the man was being very careful indeed.

Father Callahan cleared his throat, and Ben pulled himself out of his head.

"Ben, I think I should tell you a story. One that I heard a long time ago, but I believe has suddenly become important." He paused, and Ben waited for him to catch his breath. "But not here. Not in this place. Does Seaforth have a parish?"

Ben nodded.

"Yeah, it hasn't been used in years, though. After the last riot, we shut it down. Inmates were using it as a safe spot to exchange letters, contraband, you name it. And Father Regis was either turning a blind eye to this or was actually contributing to it—we never found out which, but he was let go and the parish became off limits. There were some security issues with the place, too; the electronic lock kept failing. Had to replace it with an old-fashioned one."

Father Callahan frowned, but nodded. Ben also knew him to be an understanding man.

And the priest was one of the few privileged enough to know what kind of prisoners they kept at Seaforth Prison.

The worst kind.

The *Carson* kind.

"Let's go there," the elderly priest said. "And then we'll talk."

***

"When I was a much younger man, I was involved in an exorcism...one that failed. Badly. It was...very unpleasant," Father Callahan said. Nearly completely blind, the man had a way of looking off to one side as he spoke that Ben found slightly unnerving. "For a long time afterward, I searched for what happened to people after they died. As a priest, I thought I knew, but..." He shook his head. "Then a man came to my parish with two gifts and a book."

"Gifts?"

Father Callahan waved an arthritic hand.

"Another story for another time. But the book—the man also brought a book called *Inter vivos et mortuos*."

The priest waited, and eventually Ben shook his head after realizing that the man was expecting a response.

"Never heard of it."

Father Callahan tilted his head to the other side.

"No, of course not—very few have. There are not many secrets left in this world, this much you must know already, but this, the *Inter*, is one of them. And I have never told anyone about it before."

The warden reached out for his Styrofoam cup and took a sip of his now lukewarm coffee. It was too bitter, and he grimaced as he swallowed.

Ben also had his secrets, including having seen Quinn walking around after he had been murdered. He shook his head.

That wasn't real. It couldn't have been real.

"The book is all in Latin, and the pages…they were very old, nearly crumbling. It took me a long time to translate it word for word. It wasn't just what the man who gave it to me said about the book, it was also the book itself. Every time I held it, every time my fingers brushed the dark leather cover, I could feel that it had power. I didn't trust anyone to read it, so I had to learn Latin to translate it all by myself. This took time…lots of time. And without anyone else to look it over, I kept second guessing myself."

Ben took another gulp of coffee and resisted the urge to interrupt. He had no idea how this story of a book was going to help him understand what had happened to Quinn.

"I know you have things to do, Ben," Father said, as if reading his mind, "but have patience. Even as a much younger man,

you struggled with the art of just waiting and watching. You'll
see that waiting and watching will serve you very well moving
forward. Please, allow me to take my time."

Ben bit his lip and flexed his biceps involuntarily. He re-
spected and trusted Father Callahan, but as the warden at Seaforth Prison, he just wasn't used to being told what to do.

Still, he swallowed his pride and waited for the man to continue.

*Patience...like the three minutes that Carson used to tear out
Quinn's eyes.*

"*Inter vivos et mortuos* tells only one story, a simple tale of a
time where the land of the living and of the dead come close
together—where they touch. As a man of the cloth, I am a be-
liever of an eternal soul, as are you, Ben. And I *used* to believe
in a heaven and a hell. But this book, this story, if you will,
doesn't describe heaven and hell as different places, but as the
same place. And in this place, you are given a choice: to remain
whole and burn, or throw yourself into the Sea, lose your *self*,
and replenish the quiddity."

"The what?" Ben asked.

"Quiddity."

The warden shook his head. He was beginning to think that
bringing Father Callahan to Seaforth had been a bad idea. The
man was speaking as if he had some sort of dementia, an affect.

Heaven and hell as one place? Quiddity?

What did he expect the man to do here, anyway? Especially
if he wasn't willing to tell him about Quinn.

Father Callahan continued, more slowly this time.

"Doesn't matter. What matters is that this place...it used to
be a one-way street. You go there, make your decision, and
that's it. But lately, things are changing. Things are becoming
more fluid in this place. People are coming back. And if this

gate opens, the things that will flood into our world..." He paused and looked off to one side again. "Well, these things will make Carson look like a teddy bear."

"Is it like the apocalypse? Something like that?" Ben asked softly.

Father Callahan mulled this over for a moment.

"Maybe...but, to be honest, I don't know for certain. This book, this story, well, it isn't exactly in tune with the tenets of Catholicism, as you can rightly tell. But, Ben, it should be taken very, very seriously. Some of the things I have seen and heard lately, about a woman in the swamp..."

The man shook his head, his lined face sagging. When he spoke again, his voice was so low that Ben had to lean in close to make out the words.

"There is something happening to our world, Ben. Something very, very wrong."

Despite being fairly certain that the man had started to lose it, the way the words came out of the old man's mouth—with such *conviction*—chilled Ben's blood.

"What does this have to do with me, Father? What does it have to do with what happened here? With Carson?"

He thought he saw the priest swallow hard.

Was that...was that fear?

Ben couldn't be certain, but he thought that maybe it was. And this was more than enough to give Ben pause. Father Callahan could be blunt, straightforward, and honest to a fault, but one thing he never was was afraid.

Except for now.

The priest nodded slowly.

"The place is called the Marrow, Ben, and the man in charge calls himself the Goat."

Chapter 5

"THREE...NO, FOUR QUIDDITY." Allan squinted hard through the lens, which he panned about the room. "No, three."

He lowered the camera.

"Not sure, there is something strange going on with the fourth. But I know that less than nearly a year ago, there were three quiddity here, in this place. Strong ones, too. Ones that definitely left a mark."

Robert glanced quickly to Shelly and Cal. The former clearly wasn't buying any of this. Cal, on the other hand, seemed rapt with interest.

The check that Sean had given them had cashed without problem, and true to his word, Cal had started to exercise more regularly. Robert, on the other hand, was drinking more often, and the hour of his drink of choice—scotch, always scotch—kept creeping up earlier and earlier each day.

And Shelly had no problem joining him. She had joined him in a lot of things lately.

They hadn't talked that much about what had happened in the Seventh Ward; all of them just wanted to put, and leave, that horrific night behind him. But Robert had caught Cal staring at the three burn marks on his leg several times, despite wearing pants as often as possible, and he knew that his friend wasn't entirely done with quiddity or the Marrow.

And it scared him—that look scared him.

At first, Robert had tried to find Sean again, to demand answers to more questions, but the man didn't seem to exist. It was rare in this day and age that absolutely no trace of a person could be found online, but this appeared to be the case with Sean.

Leland...he's your father...

He had also searched for LBlack, but the man had gone dark. It couldn't have been him anyway, just like he couldn't be his father. He had a dad, and a mom, nice people who'd died in an accident a number of years back. And his father, Alex Watts, had never worn a jean jacket.

So Robert resigned himself to just sitting and waiting, drinking every day to help him forget about his daughter's voice, the faces in the fire.

He even tried to forget about the sand, the waves.

And that had worked surprisingly well.

Until Allan had knocked on the door a few minutes ago.

"They leave a mark? A trail of some sort?" Robert asked, his interest suddenly piqued.

Allan nodded.

"Yeah, most of the time—it depends. The longer the spirits stay here, the longer their mark stays."

"What does it mean?"

Allan shrugged.

"That's something I thought you could help me with."

"Let me ask you something, Allan," Cal interjected. "Have you ever seen a spirit—?"

"Fuck, stop calling it spirit," Shelly spat.

Cal gave her a look.

"Fine," he said slowly. "Quiddity...quid? Can we call them fucking quid, Your Highness?"

Shelly took a step forward, and Robert held up his hands.

"What the hell is going on with you guys? Just keep it together. Jesus."

Shelly's expression turned sour, but she didn't offer a retort; progress, for her.

Cal turned back to Allan.

"Have you ever found quiddity using your camera that you *can't* see with your eyes?"

Allan looked at him like he had some sort of mental deficiency.

"Yes—of course. Abut 50/50, actually. Most of the time it's after car accidents and other horrible things."

Robert took a sip of the scotch in his hand.

"What does this all have to do with us, Allan?"

"I want to help. I managed to send my parents on their way to the other side a decade ago, but I'm not really sure how I did it. And my god, they were grateful. I just want to help, is all."

Robert chewed the inside of his lip. He had tried hard to forget about this whole world and its implications.

But if this boy…if he and his strange cameras could offer a true way back, a way to get Amy back, then maybe…

Robert shook his head.

It's not possible. Sean's gone. The rest is…the rest is just a bad dream. Amy's gone. Your life is here.

"Allan," he said after a heavy sigh. "Thanks for coming, for showing us your gear. It really is fascinating, but I think you got the wrong impression about us—misinterpreted what I posted online."

Robert stood, and Allan's face drooped.

"Woah, wait a second—" Cal got to his feet as well. He indicated himself, Robert, and Shelly with a circular gesture. "We should talk about this, guys. Maybe—"

Robert shook his head.

"No, I'm done talking."

He held out his hand for Allan to shake it, and the boy tentatively extended his own.

"Robbo? This isn't—"

Robert shook Allan's hand and indicated that he should head to the door. Shelly followed closely behind the young man.

"No, Cal," Robert said sternly. "That's over—it's over. I don't know what happened to you back then, with your friend, but we're not dwelling in that world anymore."

Cal threw his hands up.

"My friend? What the *fuck* do you know about my friend?"

Robert was taken aback by his friend's sudden aggression. This wasn't the Cal that he knew, the goofy, good-natured but blunt as hell conspiracy theorist.

This was someone else.

"Nothing, but we're done—"

Cal's eyes went wide.

"Done? *Done?* Who died and made you king? What made you so fucking special, Robbo?"

A sudden pain in Robert's calf caused him to grimace and he nearly buckled.

"Fuck," he swore, bending over to massage his lower leg.

"That makes you special? Why don't you fucking tell us the truth about what happened to you in the Ward, Robbo, about how you got those scars?" He took another step forward. "While you're at it, why don't you tell Shelly about what Sean told you? Huh? Yeah, that's right, I heard what he said to you on the porch. You think I'm an idiot? You think—"

"That's enough, Cal!" Robert shouted.

"Why? Who—?"

And that was it; Robert lost it.

"It's my fucking house, so it's my fucking rules. You don't like it, Cal? Then maybe you should find another place to live. Go, get the fuck out."

Cal's eyes narrowed and he pointed a finger at Robert's chest.

"Your house? *Your* house? If it weren't for me and Shelly here, you'd be rotting in the Marrow. Fuck, we saved your ass at Pinedale, too, lest you forget that as well? So it's your place? Why? Because your name is on the deed because Sean Sommers somehow gets it signed by a dead woman? Well, fuck this."

Robert was taken aback by his friend's sudden intense anger. He turned and saw Allan staring at them both, eyes wide.

"Shelly, see Allan out, okay?"

The woman obliged by coming up behind Allan and nudging him forward.

"Time to go, li'l guy," she said softly. "Mommy and Daddy are fighting again."

"No, you know what?" Cal said, drawing Robert's gaze back. "Fuck this—you want me out? Then I'll go. I don't even want to stay here."

He finished his beer then blew by Robert, almost knocking into him in the process.

"C'mon, Allan. I'll see you out."

"Cal—"

Cal turned his back and grabbed Allan roughly by the arm. Then he held up his middle finger to Robert.

"Fuck you, Robert—fuck you with your secrets and lies and holier than thou utter *bullshit*."

And then he left with Allan, leaving Robert to stand there, his mouth agape.

What the fuck just happened?

Chapter 6

WARDEN BEN TRISTEN EXHALED slowly, then rubbed his eyes. The lighting inside the chapel was poor, and dusk seeped through the single stained-glass window above the altar. As he stared at the Jesus on the cross made of colored glass, he wondered if Father Callahan was just confused, senile even.

What about Jesus? God and all that?

Allegories, Ben; allegories for the Marrow, the Goat, the Sea.

It befuddled him that a man such as Callahan—a priest, no less—had abandoned his faith for another. But it was not for him to question, he supposed.

Ben squinted at the window, and realized that it was the only one in the entire prison that wasn't covered in bars. Then he shook his head. It didn't matter. Seaforth Prison was located on an island more than twenty miles from land. Even if one of the inmates was to escape, they couldn't go anywhere.

Lightning suddenly ripped through the sky, illuminating the crown of thorns on Jesus's head.

"So…what now?" he said after a long pause.

Father Callahan surprised him by rising to his feet.

"I need to go see the inmate—to see Carson," he said simply.

Ben eyed his old friend suspiciously. He was crooked, his spine curved like a withered branch. His eyes were a frosty white from cataracts, and his skin was like leather left in the sun for far too long.

He shook his head.

"I don't think that's a good idea, Father."

"Are you worried about me?"

Ben nodded.

"Not just you, Father. I'm worried about *anyone* going in there…you saw what Carson did to Quinn. He's going to be alone for a long, long time."

It was definitely a mistake bringing Callahan here, he realized.

Go see Carson? He is definitely off his rocker.

No way. No fucking way.

Father Callahan seemed to mull this over for a moment.

"This is bigger than me, Ben. Besides, I'm old; my time on this earth is nearly spent. It won't matter what happens to me."

Ben stood and put a gentle hand on the man's shoulder.

"I couldn't live with myself if anything happened to you, Father. I can barely—" He took a hitched breath. "I shouldn't have let anything happen to Quinn, and I won't let anything happen to any of the others."

Father grimaced.

"Ben? I don't think—"

Again, the warden shook his head.

"I want to thank you for coming out here, Father. Your presence, if nothing else, has made me feel more comfortable. And the story…thank you for sharing. One day soon we'll have a scotch and talk more about it—what was it? *Between the living and the dead?* Yeah, we'll have a good, long chat. But for now, I think it's best if you headed back to the mainland. I need to figure out how to get Quinn's body off the island."

Father Callahan reached for his cane and wrapped his gnarled hand around the handle. He took a step, with Ben's guidance, but then he stopped abruptly.

"Ben, why is it that you really called me here?"

Ben looked at his friend and hesitated.

"It wasn't just be to show me a video of your friend, Quinn, was it? I mean, I'm no psychologist, just an old, frail priest."

The warden kept tight-lipped. The way the priest was be-having, the borderline blasphemous things he was saying, it would do neither of them any good to mention what he had seen.

A smile suddenly broke on the man's lined face.

"You saw him, didn't you? You saw the man after he died."

A vision of Quinn, clutching his face as he ran into the mess hall, passed through his mind and Ben shuddered.

"Ben, please, I *must* see Carson. If you saw your friend, then things are worse than I thought. Things are accelerating. We — I — need to stop it."

Another pause.

"Ben, please."

"Suppose I believe this, Father, everything that you are say-ing, and suppose that I did see my friend's spirit. How is talking to Carson going to help? What are you going to do? How could you possibly stop him?"

"The man…the man who gave me the book, he made me a Guardian, Ben. A Guardian of the Marrow. *I* can stop Carson. It's in the *Inter vivos et mortuos*; the rift can be closed, but only by one of us. And only before it's fully open."

Ben squinted hard.

Guardian.

The stories were just getting more fantastical the longer he spoke to the priest. His friend. His friend who clearly needed help. He wished he could just take Father Callahan to speak to Carson, show him that the man was just a run-of-the-mill psy-chopath, one that oddly said similar shit to what he was saying now, and let him realize that there was no secret portal to an-other world in Cell Block E.

Sure, there was death and evil, of that Ben had no doubt. Only it came in the form of a despicable human named Carson Ford.

"No," he said simply. "I'm going to get you off the island, Father."

The man bowed his head, as if finally accepting his fate. But he wasn't done yet; not quite.

"What about the spirit of your friend, Ben? The one you saw after he died?"

Ben shook his head.

"Wasn't real, it was just stress. Now, please—"

"Your friend isn't the only dead here, Ben. I saw several others when I arrived by boat. I fear that this place—that this *prison*—has a very important role to play in this rift between worlds. Which is why I *must* speak to Carson."

Ben shook his head again.

The priest was just so certain, so convinced of his own words, that it was infectious. Flexing his biceps, Ben reverted back to his safe place. The place that he understood. The role that he had occupied for nearly two decades.

Ben Tristen was the warden of Seaforth Prison, and nothing was going to happen to anyone else while he was in charge.

"No," he said sternly. "I'm sorry, Father, but I can't let you see Carson. Again, I thank you for coming, but I must insist that you head back to the mainland now. I will arrange for the boat to pick you up."

Lightning suddenly illuminated the room again, and Ben's eyes shot to the stained-glass window.

The rain is coming.

He gently guided the priest toward the door.

"And I think we should hurry…there's a storm brewing."

Father Callahan shook Ben's hand off him and leaned on his cane.

"Indeed," he said, his croaky voice taking on a strange, distant quality. "There is a storm coming."

Chapter 7

"YOU THINK HE KNOWS about us?" Shelly asked, her hand moving gently over Robert's bare chest. Robert took a deep breath.

"You mean Allan?"

Shelly pinched him and he cringed.

"Not Allan, for fuck's sake. Cal. You think he knows?"

Robert pictured the way his friend had lost it, how he'd stormed off.

Sure, he *could* know about them, and Cal did have a jealous streak.

Why don't you tell us what Sean told you? About what really happened in the Seventh Ward?

It could also be that.

And then there were the colored streaks in Allan's camera fitted with the special lens, streaks that the quiddity had left behind.

You acting weird lately, Robbo? Getting angry more than usual?

It could be that, too.

Or it could just be Cal being Cal.

Fuck.

"Don't know, Shelly. I've known Cal for...what? Fifteen years? He's...different."

Her hand moved to his navel, sending a shiver up his spine.

"I've known him for less than a year, and you don't have to tell me that he's *different*."

Robert sighed.

Things hadn't gotten easier since the Seventh Ward; if anything, they had become more confusing.

Leland is your father...

Robert had done some research into his parents, but he hadn't been able to dig up anything of significance. His first thought was that maybe he was adopted, but he found no record of this. All evidence suggested that he was indeed the son of Alex and Helen Watts, a litigator and a homemaker. Nice people who'd done their best to raise him before tragically passing away in a car accident. And he had good memories, too. Good times playing baseball with his dad, baking cookies with Mom. But Sean's comment, as innocuous as it was, had sent a schism through his mind. Was it all fake? A fabrication?

And, more importantly, did it matter?

"What are you thinking about?" Shelly asked. She was resting her head on his chest as they lay beside each other in bed, and she turned her bright eyes up to meet his.

"Nothing," Robert lied, looking away.

"You're lying," she whispered, but then she snaked her hand below the sheets, her fingertips brushing against the inside of his thighs ever so lightly. "But that's okay, I'll give you something to think about."

She propped herself onto her elbows, then lowered her face to his. Her lips, for all of their ample size, were incredibly gentle, brushing against Robert's own like soft, velvety pillows. Then her tongue flicked out, equally as gentle, and he felt another tremor.

Shelly smiled, and her hand moved from the inside of his leg to between them.

Robert instantly hardened.

"Again?" he whispered, swallowing hard.

Shelly's smile grew, and she nodded vigorously.

"Yes, again," she said.

Robert reached over, grabbed her hips, and in one fluid motion, moved her on top of him. Then he pulled her head close and kissed her again, while at the same time slipping inside her.

Robert rolled onto his back, breathing heavily, his hair and face soaked with sweat.

"That was..."

Shelly, who had been facing away, turned and put a finger to his lips, silencing him. Her eyes were glowing, and her entire body was covered in a thin sheen.

There was no need to say it.

Then she rolled to a sitting position, and Robert marveled at her body. Even though her back was to him, he could still see the side of her large breast, the small, pink nipples still hard, and he smirked.

Shelly reached out to grab something from the floor, and Robert propped his head on his elbow and started to trace her spine with his fingers.

The first time they'd had sex had been clumsy, like fumbling teenage virgins, and it had ended far too early, for which Robert was to blame. It had been so long since he had had sex, and even when Wendy was alive, it had been strictly missionary. But with Shelly...her freedom and *experimentation* was liberating.

And it was fun, too. Something that had been sorely missing from his life before her.

The second time had been better, the third and subsequent occasions nothing short of amazing. As the endorphins flooded his system, they usurped the prickling sensation of guilt that served no other purpose but to nag him.

Unfounded feelings of guilt rooted in Wendy.

She touched him from even beyond the grave.

Shelly picked something up, and Robert tried to lean around to take a look, but she turned her back to him, blocking his view.

"What are you playing with?" he asked tentatively. He was open to newer experiences, sure, but the metallic click and subsequent whir of a tiny motor made him nervous.

He had limits—he was an accountant, after all.

"Shel?"

At first, she didn't respond. Then Robert heard another click and she spun, a camera pointed directly at him. He instinctively put his hands in front of his face.

"What, you getting shy on me, Rob?" she teased, snapping several pictures.

Robert pawed at the camera.

"Put it down, Shel. I'm serious. Not in the mood."

Shelly snapped a few more pictures.

"Shelly—I'm serious."

She lowered the camera.

"You're no fun."

Robert eyed the camera as she turned it on herself and fiddled with some of the settings. Then his brow furrowed as he recognized the reddish filter covering the lens.

"Where'd you get the camera from?"

Shelly shrugged.

"Shelly—did you take it? Did you take it from the kid?"

She flicked a button and the camera lens started to glow a dull red. Robert reached for it, but Shelly stood and moved away from him.

"Maybe," she said unapologetically.

"Shelly! You stole the boy's camera, didn't you?"

Standing nude, she aimed the camera at him again. The red light was strange, and it made Robert uncomfortable beyond the idea of being photographed immediately following sex.

"Borrowed," she said.

"Give it to me!" Robert demanded, but Shelly only laughed.

He rolled to the edge of the bed and stood. As the sheet fell away, he suddenly felt self-conscious and tried to cover himself. Shelly continued to laugh as she lowered the camera toward his flaccid penis. He covered himself with both hands, but Shelly just continued to pan up and down his body with the strange red light.

"You really think that the nerdy kid can see spirit trails with this thing?"

"I don't care, Shelly. Just turn it off—it's making me uncomfortable."

But Shelly didn't turn it off; instead, she panned all the way down his body. But when she reached his calves, the smile on her face suddenly fell away.

Shelly finally lowered the camera, giving Robert a clear view of her now pale face.

"Shel? What's wrong?"

The woman swallowed hard, but didn't reply. Instead, she slowly extended a finger and pointed at his injured calf.

Chapter 8

WARDEN BEN TRISTEN FOLLOWED closely behind Father Callahan as they made their way from the parish down the long hall toward the front gates. Guard John Smitts followed behind Ben.

It had been two days since Quinn's murder, and since then no one had been permitted to speak to Carson. Food delivery was done by guards wearing headphones.

Ben had absolutely forbidden any contact.

The other twenty-two prisoners had been confined to their single-person cells for the foreseeable future, and they had started to become antsy.

The rest of Ben's staff, aside from the ten guards and the IT guy that Ben thought had severe autism, had been moved off the island for safety reasons.

All of his actions had rendered the long, featureless hallway that separated the prison from the front door, a thirty-foot passage marked by cameras in all four corners, strangely quiet.

That is, until the walkie on Ben's belt crackled and squawked. Everyone save Father Callahan jumped—they were all on edge given the events of the past few days.

Ben unhooked the walkie from his belt and pressed the talk button.

"Yeah—Warden here."

More static.

"Who is this?"

Ben stared at the small plastic box in his hand for a moment before answering.

"What are you talking about? You called me—it's the Warden."

"Oh." There was a short pause, and Ben waited patiently for the man to continue. "Well, it's Petey...checked out the weather patterns, we've got a 10-beller rollin' in. If you wanna get the package out, gotta do it pronto, Chief."

Ben shook his head, trying to decipher his head of IT's bizarre lingo and even stranger behavior.

Package...Father Callahan? Or Quinn's body? Both had to leave today. 10-beller must be a heavy storm.

"Copy that. We're on our way out now. What's the storm look like? Last a day?"

Father Callahan's pace, snail-like to begin with, slowed even more. Ben laid a hand gently on his shoulder, encouraging him to keep moving.

"A day? No way, Chief. It's gonna last three days, maybe even four. If the patterns stay like this, it's gonna be detention, looks like."

Detention?

Ben grimaced.

"For fuck's sake, Peter, what do you mean detention? This is a fucking prison...speak English."

"Sorry, Chief. Meant that no one is gonna be able to come and go until the storm passes. Good thing you got the cooks and nurses off the island. On second thought, maybe the nurses..."

Peter's ramblings trailed off and the warden swore under his breath. They approached the thick metal door at the front, and he bobbed a head at Smitts, a man that was nearly as large and muscular as Ben himself, with a square jaw and shaved head.

"Get the door, Smitts," he instructed.

John Smitts, an ex-con before turning to this side of the law, retrieved the keys from the ring on his belt and started to unlock the heavy latch. A year ago, a mandate had come down from the board that everything at Seaforth had to go electronic, which was mostly fine by Ben. But he was a bit of a traditionalist, and he put his foot down when it came to this door, the inner entrance to Seaforth Prison.

For whatever reason, it just felt safer with an old-fashioned lock and key.

But as Quinn found out, it was the dangers inside that they had to worry about.

"Chief?"

As Smitts fiddled with the lock, the large metal key banging loudly, Ben pressed the talk button on the walkie again.

"Copy that." The static from the walkie reminded him of the video from Cell Block E and how it had gone pure white noise for three minutes. Peter hadn't been able to find the source of the malfunction, despite all his glowing gadgets and computers. "And Peter? Do a full system rundown, don't want anything cutting out like—" He caught himself before he said, *the night that Quinn died.* "—a couple nights ago. You got that? No down time."

"Gotcha, Chief."

Smitts opened the door, and the four of them entered into a small square room. This room was the first layer of security for Seaforth. Smitts waited for Ben and Father to enter before closing and locking the door to the hallway that they had just come through. Neither door could be opened—the first leading to the outside, or the interior one leading to the prison—unless the other was both closed and locked.

"And Peter?"

"Yeah?"

"Don't call me Chief—I'm not a fucking Indian, and this is no Pow-Wow. Call me Warden."

"Alrighty, Chi—I mean Warden."

Ben sighed and turned the walkie volume down.

"Smitts, where's the body?"

The man, who rarely spoke unless asked a direct question, had a voice like rusted nails.

"Brought it out earlier. Wrapped in the tarp like you asked. Should be right outside the door, Hargrove is out there with it, ready to escort Quinn and Father to the boat."

Ben nodded, then he stepped forward and pulled the keycard from his belt, ready to open the front door.

"Warden? Shouldn't we…?" Smitts let his sentence trail off.

Ben eyed him suspiciously.

Shouldn't we what?

Then the man nodded toward Father Callahan, who was standing still, facing the front door of the prison.

Ben made a face, realizing what his guard was hinting at: it was protocol to search everyone who came and left the prison. His gaze went to the old, tired priest.

"It's fine, Smitts," Ben said, bringing the keycard up to the unit and activating it. Then he stepped backward, looking directly into the camera that whirred as it focused on him.

C'mon, Peter, we just fucking spoke.

A second later, a loud buzz filled the small room, and the sound of the outer lock disengaging could be heard. The warden waited for it to finish before shoving the door wide.

The salty brine of the sea hit him in the face and he experienced a sharp intake of breath. His eyes immediately darted upward.

Peter wasn't kidding about the storm.

The sky was dark, nearly black, despite being half past noon. Thick, menacing-looking clouds blanketed out the sun.

"Fuck me," Ben whispered. When he turned, he was surprised that Father Callahan was staring directly at him. He started to blush. "Here, Father. Take my hand."

The man ignored the gesture.

"I'm slow and nearly blind, but I'm not feeble," he said matter-of-factly.

Ben withdrew the gesture, shrugged, then he turned his eyes to the sea, which was frothing into a frenzy. The front doors to Seaforth Prison opened to a long concrete pathway that led down the forty or so feet to sea level. At the bottom, he could see the faint outline of the tug.

The wind howled, whipping against his face, and the warden tucked his head into his considerable shoulders.

"Smitts?" he asked, his eyes on the boat as it swayed and rocked in the waves.

"Yeah?"

"Where's Hargrove?"

A man suddenly appeared from behind a shrub, a cigarette dangling from the corner of his mouth.

"Right here," he said, a goofy grin on his face. "Just had to take a piss."

Ben nodded.

"And Quinn? Where's Quinn's body?"

Hargrove hooked a thumb over his shoulder.

"Already loaded up. Took the poor bastard down earlier." The man turned his small eyes skyward. "Gonna *fucking* pour. Need to get going quick. Weather is even worse on the mainland."

Ben nodded, his expression stern.

"Take Father Callahan back—get him a ride when you land to wherever he wants to go, as well. And then I want you back here, Hargrove—I need you back here right away. The weather is supposed to be shit, so don't capsize the damn boat. But I *need* you back here."

The man nodded, took a drag, then flicked the cigarette to the ground. As he moved toward the priest to lend a hand, Ben turned toward his long-time friend.

"I want to thank you for coming, Father. And for your assistance with blessing Quinn's body. He was...he was a great friend."

Father Callahan stared at him blankly.

"I wish you would reconsider, Ben. I need to speak to *him*."

Ben caught strange looks from the other two men, but he ignored them.

"Another time, perhaps," he said with a strained smile. He nearly had to shout over the roaring wind.

Father Callahan shook his head in disgust, then turned to leave without another word.

Ben watched him go, his crooked frame leaning on Hargrove to navigate the hard concrete path. Then he turned back to face the prison, and instructed Smitts to go back inside.

Before he followed, he looked up at the imposing building.

Hard, made of solid concrete, nearly as impenetrable as a fortress, Seaforth made for a formidable appearance.

Lightning suddenly flashed, illuminating the dust-gray surface, and a chill suddenly traveled up Ben's spine.

A thick raindrop hit him on the forehead, and he hurried back inside, unable to shake the feeling that this storm was going to consist of more than just thunder, lightning, and rain.

Much, *much more.*

Chapter 9

"IT'S A FUCKING CAMERA, Shelly. Take it easy."

Shelly held the device out to him, but Robert refused to grab it from her.

"But...but your *leg*."

Robert swallowed hard, trying desperately to change the subject.

"Why are you getting all freaked out? I mean, some pipsqueak says that he can use his camera to see...what? Ghost trails? And not only do you believe him, but—"

"Just look through the lens, for fuck's sake, Robert!"

Shelly then proceeded to hold the camera at arm's length and actually dropped it.

"Fuck!" Robert fell for the ruse and reached out. The camera landed in his open palm, and he juggled it for a moment before his fingers got tangled in the strap.

He shot Shelly a look, but her face was still so pale and blanketed in concern that he couldn't hold the expression. Reluctantly, he held the camera viewfinder up to his face.

The last photograph taken was still on the screen, and Robert's breath caught in his throat.

He could see the tops of his thighs, oddly gray despite the red filter, but it was what was on his right calf that gave him pause.

The skin on his shin was taut, the back of the leg thin, bordering on polio-like. But wrapping his gray flesh were three glowing, red-and-yellow claw marks—marks from where Leland Black had cauterized his leg wound.

Robert shut off the camera and sat down on the bed, no longer self-conscious about the fact he was naked. He took several deep breaths, and then tapped the bed beside him. Lowering his head, he waited until he felt Shelly's weight press down on the mattress.

"You gonna tell me what really happened in the basement, Rob? With Dr. Mansfield?" Shelly asked softly. "If you want to keep this—"

She hesitated, then swatted at his arm, forcing him out of his own head.

"Hey, you listening to me?"

Robert looked over at her, and was surprised that there was sadness on her round face.

"If you want to keep this"—she gestured to their naked bodies—"going, you are gonna have to tell me what really happened to you. Cal's right, I don't do well with secrets, Rob."

Robert took a good long look at Shelly. It wasn't just the sex, although that was undeniably great; it was something else, too. There was just something about her, something about this foul-mouthed blonde with an attitude that he couldn't get enough of.

He liked her, he realized, maybe even loved.

Strangely, this time the characteristic pang of guilt that he usually felt never came. Robert sighed, and then started to talk.

"It happened in the basement, Shelly. And it happened again in the Seventh Ward…"

***

When he was done, Robert lowered his eyes again, content with staring at the floor by his bare feet. The story, all of the story up to what Sean had said about Leland being his father, came out in a rush. He had played this moment, the moment he shared what he knew with someone, over in his head dozens of times, and all of these times he thought it would be difficult to speak about how he felt, about his guilt, about the strangeness of the Marrow. But the reality was that it wasn't hard at all.

It helped that Shelly just listened wide-eyed the entire time.

For a full minute, neither of them said anything. They just sat there on the corner of the bed, naked, breathing deeply. Then Shelly brought a hand up and laid it gently on his shoulder. He turned to her, staring at her large eyes.

Even though it had been easier than expected to share his story, he would be lying if he said he wasn't worried about how she would take it.

"Well, that's pretty fucked up, isn't it?"

Shelly smirked when she said this, and Robert laughed—a tense, high-pitched sound.

"Yep, pretty fucked up. I'm sorry I didn't tell—"

She put her finger to his lips, shushing him.

"I get it," she said quietly. There was another pause, and she looked off to one side. "You ever wonder what it all means, Robert? And do you think it's an accident that you—*we*—got involved?"

Robert mulled this over for a second.

"I don't know. Part of me wants to think that it was all an accident—and it was, really. After all, it started with—" His breath hitched, but he forced through it. "—Wendy and Amy dying in the car accident. But Sean came to see me…he gave me the letter. *That* was no accident."

Shelly nodded.

"So what are we going to do? Keep on keeping on? Doing the same thing, each and every day?"

The question confused Robert, and he turned to face her.

"What do you mean?"

Shelly reached over and picked up the camera.

"Look, what happened here in the estate and in the Seventh Ward was fucked up—no one gets that as much as I do. But I've been doing more research, and the dweeb Allan Knox? I think he might be onto something. There is more chatter on the net, about seeing more quiddity than ever before." She paused and chewed her lip. "I don't know if it fucking means anything, but something…I dunno, something tells me that there is something important going on here. Something that we are a part of whether we want to be or not."

Robert suddenly lay down on the bed and brought his arms up and put the backs of his hands on his forehead.

He took a deep breath.

"What if I don't want to be involved? What if all I want to do is live a normal life? What if I want to forget all about these quiddity and the Marrow and all this other bullshit?"

He closed his eyes, but then opened them again when Shelly flopped down beside him.

"You know what, Robert? I didn't choose to have blonde hair, big tits, or an even bigger ass. I just got 'em. I didn't ask to be a fucking dynamo in bed. I just am."

Robert chuckled.

"Sometimes we should just roll with the punches, play poker with the cards we're dealt. We don't always get a chance to re-shuffle the deck."

Shelly propped herself onto an elbow and stared at him.

"And you, Robert, most definitely have been chosen for something bigger, something greater. The sooner you can come to terms with that, the sooner we can do something fucking *good*—something really good."

Robert shivered at the word *chosen*, recalling that Sean had used the exact same word when they had first met.

He leaned over and kissed her on the lips.

"Thank you," he said softly. Despite her crassness, her words had imbued him with a strange confidence.

Sean Sommers's influence or not, he had purged James Harlop and Andrew Shaw. *He* had done that...with the help of his friends, of course.

"What now?"

Shelly's answer was immediate.

"Now we go find that retard Cal and his nerdy boyfriend and see what kind of trouble we can get into. What do you think?"

Robert nodded.

"I think you're right."

Shelly smiled.

"Fuckin' A, I'm right. Best you remember that."

Chapter 10

"**WHAT THE FUCK?**" **BEN** said as he slurped what was left of his egg off his fork. He turned to Smitts. "You see that?"

The big man nodded.

"And you heard me say to Peter that I wanted no more blackouts, right?"

Again, the man nodded. He wasn't much on words, which was all the same to the warden. Like him, John Smitts was of a different generation, a generation that didn't think everything had to be commented on, that the world wasn't made up of verbal hashtags.

But John Smitts was the strong, silent type—with a heavy emphasis on the strong.

The lights flickered again, and Ben swore and shook his head. Lightning flashed outside, sending splinters of blue light into the mess room. Even though the activities of the inmates had been restricted and they were confined to their cells, Ben still had the freedom to roam. So after sending Callahan on his way, trying to mull over the things that he had said, he had taken Smitts to the mess hall where he had fried them both up some eggs, toasted some bread, and sat in silence.

Thinking.

Thinking about Quinn yelling at him to go, to hurry, all the while covering his face with his hands.

Thinking about the weird shit Father Callahan had said, about how he was so desperate to speak to Seaforth Prison's most dangerous inmate.

But before he had come to terms with any of this, the lights had dimmed, and now they flickered.

The warden quickly scarfed the last of his toast, cracked his swollen knuckles, then stood.

"I'm gonna have a chat with Peter."

Smitts nodded and said nothing. But the way that he quickly finished his own eggs, chasing it with a slice of bacon, indicated that he wanted to come along. Ben was happy for the company, as silent as it was.

And, besides, he was still a little freaked out at the prospect of being alone.

Of seeing Quinn again.

It wasn't real.

He took the man's plate and stacked it on his before quickly walking over to the kitchen and dropping it in one of the metal basins.

"I'll get it later," Smitts said, but Ben waved his comment away.

"Don't worry about it," Ben replied as they made their way side by side to the front of the mess hall.

The mess hall was a giant square, plain in every respect, with plastic picnic-style tables arranged in rows. It was the most dangerous part of the prison; more deaths and assaults had happened here over the last seven years than everywhere else in Seaforth combined. And that included in the workout yard.

There was just something about food and confinement that served up a toxic combination. Ben could never figure out why.

Ben's eyes drifted upward to the balcony above. Accessible only from the guards' lounge, the upper level was lined with bars, and it was typically patrolled by two officers during inmate feeding times. But now it was empty.

It was strange being on the floor with no one patrolling above. It made him uncomfortable, and he hurried to the door, where he scanned his keycard. It beeped and opened, leading to a narrow hallway. Ben went first, and Smitts followed. They passed through a metal detector, and it beeped loudly, picking up the Taser and pistol on their belts.

Ben pushed his fingers into his eyes and sighed. Fatigue was beginning to take over; he hadn't slept a wink since Quinn had been murdered.

Fucking Quinn…why did you have to go in there? What the fuck is this all about?

He thought of Father Callahan's words.

The Goat…he's saying the Goat.

Ben tried to keep his tears at bay.

Fuck, Quinn.

Ben took his hand away from his face, and turned to the camera in the upper left-hand corner of the door. He waved a hand, then stepped forward to swipe his card again.

Nothing happened.

"Fuck, Peter," he muttered.

He leaned back, staring directly up at the camera, and waved dramatically. The metal detector going off triggered the lock, but it should have also sent an alarm to Pete in the control room.

What the fuck is he doing? Sleeping?

The man crushed Red Bulls and God only knew what else, so Ben found it hard to believe that he ever slept, let alone at a time like this.

Ben pulled the walkie from his belt and turned the dial.

"Peter, open the door—metal detector went off. It's me and Smitts."

There was a pause, then a crackling voice replied.

"Chief? That you?"

Ben shook his head.

Chief.

"Yes, it's me. Open the door to the Main Block."

The pause was longer this time.

"Wave your hand, I'm having a hard time seeing you in the camera."

Ben did as he was instructed.

"Naw, still not getting it. Blurry, seems to be a weak signal or some shit."

"Fuck, just open it up, we're coming to see you anyway. The lights are flickering and—"

The door suddenly beeped and Ben heard the lock disengage. Smitts stepped forward and quickly opened it.

"Hang tight, Peter. We'll be there in five."

Then they stepped through the door and into the hallway lined with cells, where the regular population inmates were held.

Typically, opening this door was immediately met with catcalls and whoops from the gen pop. Today, however, was different. Maybe it was the news of Quinn's death, who was moderately well-liked among the inmates, or maybe it was the storm that rumbled outside.

Or maybe it was something else entirely.

All Warden Ben Tristen knew as he walked down that hallway with John Smitts at his side, glancing at the inmates in near pin-drop silence with their heads hung low, was that he didn't like it.

He didn't like it one bit.

Silence in a prison was never good.

Chapter 11

IT WAS DARK, BUT not so dark that Robert was completely blind. He seemed to be in some sort of room, but he couldn't seem to locate the walls...everything just receded into blackness at the periphery of vision. He tried to look down, but his head and eyes moved slowly. When he finally managed to focus, he realized that he was floating; either that or the ground was so dark and black that he couldn't see it.

A gasp escaped him, the sound impossibly loud in this otherwise vacuum of space.

What is this place?

He closed his eyes, and somehow managed to lower his heart rate. Then he concentrated, trying to will everything all away.

Only he couldn't manage. A voice suddenly flashed in his mind, and his eyes popped open.

You were chosen, Robert. Leland Black is your father.

It was Sean Sommers's voice.

Robert closed his eyes again.

When he opened them a second later, he was shocked to discover that he was no longer in the infinite black box, but in some sort of cell.

Only he wasn't *really* there; it was as if he were just observing.

There was a nude man in the center of the room, seated like a yogi, eyes closed. He had a strong jawline and a nose that was slightly off-center, and although Robert was positive he had never seen him before, he seemed oddly familiar to him.

There was a sort of aura coming off of him, seemingly secreted by his every pore. Something that told Robert that this wasn't a *good* man.

On the contrary, this was something completely different.

Evil, maybe.

Is this a quiddity? Some lost, dead soul?

But before he could contemplate this further, the man's lips started to move and Robert strained to hear what he was saying.

At first, Robert couldn't make it out; it just seemed to be a mindless stream of syllables repeated over and over again, but when he concentrated even further, it started to make sense to him.

It wasn't a word, but a *name*. A name that sent a shiver up his spine.

"Leland Leland Leland Leland..."

Robert swallowed hard, his mind struggling to grasp what was going on.

But what came next was even more shocking.

A response.

"The man of the cloth is coming, Carson. You can use him to open the rift—bind him between the living and the dead, just like the book says."

Robert's breathing was coming in shallow bursts now.

Unlike the man sitting cross-legged in the center of the cell, this was the voice of a man he recognized.

It was Leland Black's voice, the Goat's voice.

His *father's* voice, if Sean was to be believed.

Robert tried to lean in even closer, but the man named Carson's eyes snapped open, and Robert screamed.

***

"Wake up! Robert, wake the fuck up!"

Robert cried out and opened his eyes.

Shelly was crouched over him, her face nearly as pale as when she had put makeup on and pretended that Ruth Harlop was still alive.

"Wha—what happened?" He blinked several times, trying to clear his vision. He went to sit up, but lost his balance and fell back down on the bed again.

Shelly breathed a sigh of relief.

"Fucking hell! What happened to you?"

Robert squinted at her.

"That's what I asked you…the last thing I remember is that we were talking, and then—" He let his sentence trail off, remembering the words that he had heard Leland Black mutter.

The man of the cloth is coming, Carson.

He swallowed and brought a hand to his forehead. His skin was damp and clammy.

Who the fuck is Carson?

"Yes?" Shelly demanded. "We were fucking talking and then you just kinda collapsed onto the bed. Swooned like a teenage girl at a Bieber concert. Seriously, what the fuck is wrong with you?"

Robert licked his dry lips, but made no effort to sit up again.

"How long was I out?"

Shelly leaned away and began to put on her underwear, which were in a heap at the end of the bed.

"I dunno. Thirty seconds, maybe?"

Now Robert did sit up.

"What? *Thirty seconds?* That's it?"

Shelly stood and pulled up her underwear. Robert barely noticed that they were a lacy black G-string. She shrugged, and then moved to her shirt next.

"Yeah, maybe more. A minute, tops."

Robert's eyes narrowed. It felt like he had been in the black room for an hour, and with the man, with *Carson*, for at least that long—everything moved so slowly.

"What, you have a dream or something? Pass out?" A wry smile passed over her red lips. "Sex too fucking good for you, Robbie?" Then her face got serious. "Fucking scared me. Don't do that again."

Robert shook his head.

"I had—" he started, his heart skipping a beat as he recalled Carson's pale blue eyes.

Shelly finished putting on her shirt and then sat beside him.

"What? What was it?"

Robert shook his head.

"I think...I *don't* think it was a dream. It was more like I was peeking in on someone—someone...*bad*."

He looked up and stared at Shelly for a moment before continuing.

"I think we should find Cal, ASAP. I think we might—"

But a knock at the front door, a heavy, resounding pounding, cut him off.

Shelly grinned and she patted him on the back.

"Speak of the devil." She stood and made her way to the bedroom door, bending down to pick up his jeans on the way. She turned and tossed them at him. "Get dressed. No need for Cal to see you this way. It's bad enough I have to."

The jeans hit Robert in the chest, but he made no effort to catch them.

"Cal has his own keys, Shel. It's not him."

Chapter 12

"SO? WHAT'S GOING ON with the lights?"

The three men were standing in the control room, an isolated area in a tower that was only accessible by a guarded staircase. Circular in nature, the room had a wall of computer screens, monitors of all kinds, lining nearly half of the interior surface. There was a myriad of other computer equipment in the room, blinking lights that were all German to Ben. His eyes darted from screen to screen, narrowing as the monitors slowly grew riddled with snow, before becoming crystal clear again.

"And the monitors? What's up with them?"

Peter Granger swung around in his high-backed leather chair, which looked as new as the computer equipment, a pen clenched between his teeth. He was a thin man, with closely cropped brown hair, a pointy nose, and large brown eyes. When Ben had first hired him—or, more specifically, when the board had 'recommended' Peter to Ben—he had been a polite, sociable man, which had flown in the face of expectation. Since that time roughly three years ago, Peter had regressed somewhat, becoming more introverted, but Ben chalked this up to natural consequence of being trapped up here, alone, for nearly 24 hours a day.

Ben's eyes flipped to the garbage on the man's desk, and a frown formed on his face. There were at least a half-dozen empty Redbull cans along with shiny wrappers from a myriad of energy bars.

"Who? What?" Peter asked.

Ben's frown deepened as he stared at the man's pinprick pupils.

"Jesus—how long you been up here?"

When the man just stared, Ben shook his head.

"Never mind. What's wrong with the lights? The monitors?"

Peter blinked twice, and then seemed to snap out of his stupor.

"Dunno," he replied with a shrug.

"Take that pen out of your mouth when you're talking to me," Ben snapped, unimpressed with the man's casualness.

Peter obliged, his eyebrows lowering. His tone took on a more serious note when he spoke next.

"I have run every diagnostic I can think of and nothing has popped up yet. Best I can think is that the"—he pointed to a monitor of the outside of Seaforth Prison and the dark brooding clouds, brimming with imminent precipitation and the sea that splashed up against the rocks—"storm has some sort of pent-up electrical component."

Ben scowled.

"Electrical storm?"

He didn't like the sound of that. Unruly prisoners? He could deal with them. Even organized riots could also be dealt with.

But an 'electrical storm'? That was something out of his reach.

Ben cracked his knuckles, wincing at the pain that radiated from his swollen joints.

"Can you do anything about it?"

Peter shook his head.

"The storm?"

Ben made a face.

"No, not the storm. I mean about the lights, the monitors." Ben still had the uncomfortable sensation in his gut, something that told him that this storm and Carson were somehow related. His hand snaked into the neck of his shirt and he fondled the cross that hung there absently.

The strange words that Father Callahan had uttered still echoed in his mind.

"I've checked the generators, checked the backup batteries, put in some extra redundancies. I think—shit, *none* of this"—he gestured at the static that suddenly appeared across all dozen or so monitors—"should be happening. But I did everything I could to make sure that there are no major interruptions." He shrugged. "What else can I do?"

Ben nodded, his face still stern. He glanced at Smitts, who was standing behind him, arms crossed over his chest.

"And Carson? What's he doing?"

Ben turned back to Peter, who flicked a switch and the interior of Carson's cell appeared in the center monitor.

The man was sitting cross-legged in the center of his room, eyes closed, hands resting gently on his knees. He wasn't wearing any clothes.

"Where're his clothes?"

Peter used the pen to point to the lower left-hand corner of the room.

"There."

Ben nodded.

He felt hatred staring in that man's face. Hatred for what he had done to Quinn, and the others he had killed.

Quinn...

A thought came over him then.

"Smitts, give us a second, would you?"

Smitts, who was staring at Carson on the monitor, a scowl on his face, suddenly snapped to.

"Warden?"

Ben nodded.

"Just give us a moment, will you?"

A dubious expression crossed the man's stern face, and Ben could have sworn that he saw the man's jaw clench. Smitts hesitated, and then nodded before turning and using his keycard to exit the room. The window in the door was filled with his back as he leaned up against it.

"Peter, I want you to do me a favor."

The man looked up at him expectantly.

"Can you roll back to two nights ago? To when Quinn was killed?"

Peter swallowed hard.

"I tried to recover the film of that, Warden, but—"

Ben shook his head.

"No, not of Cell Block E."

"Okay..."

"Can you find footage of me leaving my office and heading to the block—through the mess hall?"

Peter put the pen back in his mouth, and at first Ben thought that he was going have to provide more of an explanation. But the man quickly swiveled and turned his attention to his computer. Then he began clacking away at his keyboard, and the real-time CCD cameras from inside the prison switched to the smaller monitors that flanked the large, central one.

The big screen momentarily went dark, and then Peter pulled up a bunch of folders with different time-logs. A few more clicks, and then Ben was in the awkward position of seeing himself, sitting pensively in his worn chair, staring off into space.

"Here it is," Peter said, leaning back again. "You want me to..."

Ben shook his head.

"No, stay here."

His heart started to thump harder in his chest, pumping blood throughout his body, flushing his muscles with adrenaline.

It was just stress—Quinn wasn't there. It wasn't his spirit. Father Callahan was wrong, he's off his meds.

But he had to know.

Warden Ben Tristen leaned over Peter, his swollen fingers gripping the back of the man's chair.

He watched himself startled when the phone rang, then the subsequent one-sided conversation.

"Any audio?" he asked.

Peter shook his head.

"No audio on these cameras."

Ben nodded and turned back to the monitor, watching himself as he bolted from the room.

"Follow me," he instructed, and Peter flipped the image to another camera.

He caught sight of the back of his uniform as he ran through the gen pop area, then into the mess room. The camera switched again, and as Ben watched himself near the door to Cell Block E, where he recalled seeing Quinn clutching his face, he felt sweat begin to form on his brow.

And there was now a lump in his throat that wouldn't go down no matter how many times he swallowed.

And then there he was...or *wasn't*.

Ben watched himself on screen slow, turn his head ever so slightly, and then pause before continuing down the hallway.

There was no Quinn.

Ben exhaled slowly, and he released his grip on the back of Peter's chair.

"Pause it," he said, his voice hoarse.

Peter obliged.

"Is there anything—?"

Ben hushed him.

"Go back a few seconds," he instructed. The imaged jogged backward. "Wait! Stop there."

Ben leaned in even closer, and he could have sworn that he saw himself turn his head, and even his lips move.

What the hell? What—or who*—am I talking to?*

"Peter, no audio on this either?"

"No, no audio."

Ben closed his eyes and then gently massaged his temples.

What are you trying to prove, Ben? What's the point of this? Quinn is dead, you didn't see him.

Eyes still closed, he reached for the cross around his neck again.

You shouldn't have sent Father Callahan away. His story...there is something going on here. It's all related somehow.

Ben just couldn't shake the feeling.

"Alright, this is the best I got."

Ben's eyes snapped open, and he found himself staring not at the center screen anymore, but when he was trapped in his thoughts, his gaze had drifted slightly.

Now he was looking at the live feed from just outside the front door of Seaforth Prison.

And goddamn him if there wasn't a person trying to get in.

"Want me to—?"

"What the fuck?" Ben whispered, leaning close to the smaller screen. "Who is that!"

"What? Who?"

Ben pointed at the monitor.

"There, right fucking there! There is someone coming up to the door."

The pen fell out of Peter's mouth.

"Shit, you're right."

The man leaned forward and hammered on his keyboard. The small image was instantly transferred over to the main monitor, and all of the air was forced out of his lungs in an audible *whoosh*.

"Father Callahan?" he whispered.

"Yeah, that's him all right. I thought—"

But the words were taken from Peter's mouth as the power blinked out and the room went completely dark.

Chapter 13

EVEN BEFORE ROBERT OPENED the door to the Harlop Estate, he knew deep down who was going to be standing there. What he didn't expect, however, was the look of fear plastered on the man's square face.

"Robert," the man said, a lit cigarette dangling from his lips. "I need to talk to you."

Robert's eyes narrowed as he examined the man standing before him. On the two previous occasions that they had met, the man's short-cropped hair had been neat bordering on perfect, his suit and tie impeccable. Now, however, it looked like he hadn't slept in days; his hair was a mess, his tie loose, the top button of his shirt undone.

After their previous encounter, Robert had vowed that if he ever saw Sean again, he would tear a strip off him, let him know what he really thought about the man.

But this...this was completely, wholly unexpected. And coupled with the strange daydream that he had just had, Robert knew that this wasn't a meeting that was going to end as innocuously as a letter handed to him.

This was about something bigger, something far more important than a hundred-year-old estate and a hundred grand.

Robert stepped to one side and indicated that the man should enter. He hesitated and his eyes drifted over Robert's shoulder.

"Shelly," he said, with a simple nod. Shelly didn't return the gesture.

"This is Sean," Robert said in the form of a hackneyed introduction. "He's the guy that gave me the letters. Told me about Leland—claims that he's my dad."

Sean raised an eyebrow at this. Clearly, he wasn't expecting Robert to share this information with her.

"Yeah, like the same way that Ruth was your aunt?" Shelly said, repeating the same words that she had used earlier when Robert had first told her about what Sean had said.

What do you really know about Sean Sommers? You look at me with such disdain...

For a second, nobody said anything, and Robert fretted that they were locked in a perpetual stalemate. But then he remembered Leland's haunting words from his dream.

Father or not, the man could not be allowed to cross over into this world.

"Shel, ple—"

But he didn't have to finish his sentence. The woman scowled, bowed her head, and stepped out of the way. Only then did Sean take a final haul of his cigarette, flick it away, and then step inside the Harlop Estate. The man loosened his tie even further before looking up at Robert.

"You got something to drink?"

***

"There is...there is a rift developing in the Marrow," Sean Sommers said, his eyes focused on the golden-brown scotch at the bottom of his glass. "You've seen it, Robert. You've seen the evil there, in the flames. You've seen *him*, too."

Robert eyed the man. He seemed very different from the other times that they had met.

"But it wasn't all bad," Robert said, remembering how fulfilled he had felt on the shores. "Not everything about the Marrow is bad, is it?"

Sean shook his head.

"It's complicated, but the only quiddity that survive are the evil ones, the ones obsessed with the *self*, with their identity."

Robert frowned.

"I don't understand..."

Sean took a sip before continuing. A large sip, one that made his considerable Adam's apple bob.

"That's not important now; what's important is that Leland only wants one thing. He wants to open a rift between his world and ours. He wants to come *back*, and that cannot happen. If it does..." Sean allowed his sentence to trail off.

"The quiddity, the faces in the flames, they'll be back here?" Robert asked quietly. Just the thought of the faces morphing in and out of the fire was enough to make his palms sweat. "In our world?"

Sean nodded.

Shelly scoffed, a sound that shocked Robert into turning.

"And how the fuck do you know this shit? Hmm?"

Sean didn't hesitate.

"Because it was in the book."

Now it was Robert's turn to look incredulous. He had scoured the Internet for weeks searching for information about the Marrow, and not once had he come across the mention of any book.

"Book?"

"Book," he affirmed with a nod. "It's called *Inter vivos et mortuos*, and it describes a time when the Marrow opens up, and the horrors are unleashed on all of us."

"Oh, fuck this shit," Shelly exclaimed, throwing up her arms. "I get that there's something going on here, but this? What you're talking about? This is bullshit religious mumbo-jumbo." She turned her back to them and went to grab another beer. "Really? Lemme guess, a Jewish guy puts some fucking foliage on his head and ends up sunning himself high up on some wooden light poles? Turns some water and grapes into a shitty Merlot? That sound about right?"

"Shel—"

"Don't fucking Shel me, Robert." She gestured toward Sean. "Who is this fucking guy, huh? Why are you listening to him? Seriously, Robert, what do you really *know* about him?"

Sean went back to being stone-faced during the outburst.

"Shel—"

She held a finger out at him, and Robert stopped speaking.

Shelly was right, of course. Their eyes locked, and Robert felt his mouth go slack. He didn't know what to say.

"Well?" she demanded.

Robert shook his head, and then slowly turned back to Sean.

"Who *are* you, Sean? Who the hell are you?"

Sean finished his scotch.

"I am nobody."

Shelly scoffed angrily from behind Robert, but he ignored her.

"Oh, riddle me this, Batman."

He heard the sound of her beer being opened.

Sean sighed heavily.

"There is no time for this, Robert."

"Why?" he asked reactively. "What's the rush?"

"I think you know."

Shelly laughed.

"Fucking guy."

"Shelly's right. You need to stop talking in riddles. If you want us for...for what? What do you want us for?"

"You, not us," Sean corrected him, his gaze never straying. "And I think you know."

Robert felt his temperature rise.

"No, sorry—I have no fucking clue. Why don't you enlighten me?"

Again, Sean sighed, this time his entire body seeming to collapse at the end of it.

"Because of Carson," he said, and Robert felt his entire body go cold.

The man of the cloth is coming, Carson. You can use him to open the rift—bind him between the living and the dead, just like the book says.

"Because Carson is going to open the gateway between our worlds. He's going to let Leland out."

Chapter 14

A SCREAM RANG OUT, but the sound barely registered with Carson Ford, sitting cross-legged in the center of his cell, his nude body marred by streaks of blood and purple bruises from when the guards had beat him.

But like the fact that the lights above had blinked out, and the shouts that now filled the prison, Carson paid them no heed.

Eyes closed, he took a deep breath in through his nose, inflating his lungs to their fullest. Then he let the air out in a thin stream.

Carson let his mind go blank, drawing himself inward. Years of time in isolation had taught him to focus, to drown out everything in his mind, to shut off the prefrontal cortex.

To activate other parts of his mind.

A deeper blackness than Seaforth Prison enveloped Carson, and he slowly began to disassociate with his body. He allowed this darkness to fall over him, reveling in its velvety texture.

Time passed; how much, he knew not.

And then, in the darkness, he saw a speck of light. Only a tiny speck at first, but as he deepened into his meditation, it began to grow. And with this growth came additional details, features in the light.

It was a fire, and it burned hot.

Carson's mind was in the Marrow.

Did you do that? he thought. In this place, there was no need to speak.

I'm getting stronger, my reach expanding even further. But I need you to do the rest, a man answered.

It was the same man that had entered his head all those years ago, encouraging him to grab the knife and drive it into his stepfather's chest as soon as the man had finished putting out his cigar on his arm.

It was the man that had first introduced himself as Leland, but who Carson now referred to as the Goat.

It was the man who was going to free him from this place, and free all others like him.

The book. The man of the cloth.

That's right, Carson. As we discussed.

There was a short pause as Carson's mind moved upward, focusing on the faces in the flames. The roiling embers revealed a friend of his, Buddy Wilson, who had been convicted in Texas for crimes that rivaled his own.

And in Texas, they had the death penalty.

In New Jersey, in Seaforth, they did not.

And the man? Is he coming too?

Leland's form suddenly materialized, his faded jean jacket slowly becoming solid, as did his wide-brimmed hat. In front of him stood a young girl maybe nine or ten years old, with long blonde hair. Her heart-shaped face was aimed at the black tar-like substance on which they stood.

He'll come. He can't stay away any longer.

Leland stroked the girl's dark hair.

And when he comes to Seaforth, you know what you have to do?

If he'd had his physical form, Carson Ford would have nodded. But in this place, in this capacity, he only had his mind.

Yes. I know what to do with both him and the man of the cloth.

Leland pushed the brim of his hat, revealing his chin and a thin, lipless smile. Inside, were hundreds of pointed teeth.

Good. Don't let me down like the others, Carson. Don't let me down.

Part II – The Warden and his Cross

Chapter 15

"THERE HAVE BEEN MANY notorious murders and psychopaths in our time," Sean said as he, Rob, and Shelly sat in the Harlop living room. "Bundy, Berkowitz, Manson. But Carson Ford was—*is*—probably one of the worst...you may have heard of him?"

Robert shook his head, and glanced over his shoulder at Shelly, who did the same.

Sean grimaced.

"Really? Just completely numb to violence? These days, terrorists are the only evil that get TV time, I guess. Anyways, Carson was arrested three years ago and convicted of murdering three people, two of whom were his parents. Those crimes were committed a decade ago. There are rumors that he and a partner, Buddy Wilson, killed more than thirty people over a ten-year period."

Robert swallowed hard.

"What about these two men? Why did I have a...uh...a dream about Carson?"

Sean tugged at his tie, loosening it even further.

"Buddy's dead—executed by the state of Texas after being convicted of murdering two teenage girls. Expedited the process...no one wanted that man alive. They tried to get Carson for the same crimes, but he fought extradition. Now he's holed up at Seaforth Prison, which—"

"Seaforth Prison?" Shelly interjected. "Never heard of it."

"Not surprised that you haven't heard about that, either. It's an island prison located off the coast of New Jersey. Houses some local heroes, let me tell you. The place was set up nearly fifty years ago, but has only been occupied for less than half of that time. With the overpopulation of prisons by mostly non-violent drug offenders, the governor got sick and tired of a father of three who was incarcerated for selling a dime bag of marijuana being gutted in the showers by a mass murderer. So he moved the most dangerous offenders to Seaforth."

Robert nodded, remembering the briny smell that he had picked up along with the body sweat from the naked man sitting on the floor.

"Which is where Carson is."

Sean nodded.

"Carson is the worst of the worst."

Shelly exhaled loudly.

"Okay, fuck. What the shit does this have to do with us?"

Sean hooked a chin at Robert.

"You want to tell her? Or should I?"

"Tell her what? I don't know—"

"A couple of nights ago, I got word from an insider at the prison. Carson murdered one of the guards, somehow lured him into his cell and tore his eyes right out of his head with his bare hands."

"Jesus," Shelly whispered. She shook her head. "Fucked up, but I still don't understand what this has to do with us? Is the man he murdered still wandering the halls?"

Sean shrugged.

"Maybe, but that's not the reason why I'm here."

He paused and Shelly turned to Robert.

"Then why *are* you here?"

Robert cleared his throat, but the words still came out tight, constricted.

"The Goat."

Shelly was incredulous.

"The *what*?"

Robert turned to face his lover, his skin ashen. He didn't have to say anything; instead, he just slowly raised his right pant leg, revealing the missing muscle and the three claw marks that marked his skin.

Shelly turned equally as pale.

"What about him?" she asked softly.

Sean finished his scotch and stood.

"Carson has somehow been in contact with Leland." He turned to Robert. "He's been talking to your father, and he's planning on bringing the Marrow to us."

Robert shook his head.

"He's not my father…my father's name was Alex Watts, not Leland Black. I remember him, as I do my mother."

Sean stood and moved across to Robert, who remained seated.

"You need to remember, Robert. We need you to remember."

And then he reached out and placed both hands on Robert's forehead before he could pull back.

Shelly shouted something, but the words were drawn out like cries underwater.

And then Robert Watts's world went black.

Chapter 16

"TURN THEM BACK ON!" the warden shouted as he fumbled with the flashlight attached to his belt.

"I…I *can't*," Peter yelled. He clacked away at his keyboard, but the monitors, and the entire room, remained pitch black.

"Fuck!"

Ben finally managed to yank the flashlight from his belt and he switched it on. The room was suddenly blindingly bright, and Ben lowered the beam for a moment to allow his eyes to adjust. Still, even in the short amount of time that it was aimed at Peter, he noted that the man's face had become even paler—if that was even possible—and he was busy typing away at the keyboard with both hands.

And yet nothing happened.

"Peter? What the fuck—"

But a sound at the door interrupted him. Ben whipped around, leading with the flashlight. It was what he *didn't* see that made his heart sink.

Smitts's back was no longer blocking the window.

"Smitts!" Ben yelled. "Smitts!"

There was another cry from outside the door, only this time it was deeper, more guttural.

Ben swallowed hard, and he turned back to Peter.

"Peter what the fuck are you doing? Turn the goddamn lights back *on!*"

"I'm fucking trying!" the man shouted back, sweat dripping from his forehead.

There was another scream and a thump from somewhere in the stairwell.

"What was that?" Peter asked, his voice wavering.

Ben reached out and laid a heavy hand on Peter's shoulder.

"Peter, turn the—"

The lights suddenly flickered back on, and Ben looked upward, his grip on Peter's narrow shoulder lightening.

"Fucking hell."

Peter leaned back in his chair, a strange expression on his face.

"I didn't do anything."

Ben lowered his gaze.

"What do you mean?"

The man shrugged.

"There was no power, I couldn't—"

A wet smacking sound at the door cut Peter off, and both men turned toward the noise. Ben felt the breath forced from his lungs.

A hand was splayed across the glass—a *big* hand, one that left a trail of blood as it slowly drifted down the pane.

Ben immediately rushed to the door.

"Check the cameras, Peter! Make sure the cameras are back on and that the cells are still locked!" Ben hollered. He flashed his keycard and yanked the handle.

He almost smashed his head into it when it failed to open.

"What the fuck?"

As he swiped his keycard again, he turned his attention to the glass, looking downward. He could see Smitts lying on the ground, clutching his chest. His face was pale, his eyes closed.

Blood had started to pool beneath his body.

"Smitts!" Ben shouted, heaving on the door handle again. "Smitts, what the fuck happened? Goddammit, Peter, what the fuck is wrong with the door? *Peter!*"

"I'm trying! I don't know what happened...the power must have reset the key codes. Lemme..."

"Fuck!" Ben swore, swiping his card like a madman over the reader again and again. The result was always the same: nothing happened; the lock didn't disengage.

Ben stood there helplessly, slamming his palms against the glass, while Smitts lay dying on the ground less than a foot away.

What the fuck happened to him?

"Smitts," he said, trying to remain calm while Peter fixed the doors. The man's eyes fluttered. Ben wasn't sure if he could hear him, but now that the rest of the prison had quieted down, he thought it was worth a try. His hand instinctively went to the cross as he spoke.

What the fuck was Callahan doing back here? What in God's name is happening at Seaforth?

"Smitts, tell me what happened. Who did this to you?"

To his surprise, Smitts pulled one of the arms that was wrapped around his stomach away and held an outstretched finger down the staircase.

Ben moved as far as he could to one side, pressing his face against the cool glass as he peered down the stairs.

And then he saw it—or, more specifically, he saw *him.*

Carson's face was staring up at him, a smile on his lips. Ben stumbled backward, and when he regained control and rushed back to the glass, Carson was gone.

"I think—I think I almost—"

Ben backpedaled until he bumped into the back of Peter's chair. The man was jostled, and his fist came down hard on the keyboard.

"What?" he demanded as he turned in his chair. "What is it, Chief?"

Ben pointed toward the door, not terribly unlike how Smitts had pointed down the stairs just moments ago.

"It's Carson," he mumbled. "Carson's out. Peter, lock down the prison. Shut Seaforth off from the rest of the world."

Chapter 17

THE MASSIVE DOOR TO the church swung open, and the boy stared up at the priest in the long, flowing robes who gazed out into the hot summer air. Almost immediately, he could see sweat begin to form on the man's brow, and he gently brushed it away with the back of his hand.

"Yes?" he asked firmly.

The man that was holding the boy's hand, a man with blond hair and a square jaw that matched the shape of his head, took a drag from his cigarette before answering.

"Father Callahan?"

"Yes," the priest said again.

"I've heard about you."

Father Callahan took a deep breath before answering. A flicker of movement at eye level drew the boy's attention. There was a girl about his age standing behind the priest. She was looking at him, a severe expression on her smooth face.

Hi, the boy mouthed.

The girl didn't acknowledge him.

The priest must have noticed his interest, as he turned his head around.

"Get back downstairs, Kendra," he said gently. Then they waited in silence until her soft footsteps receded out of earshot.

"Officer, I think you should know that—"

The blond man shook his head, and then reached up to adjust the tie that hung around his neck.

"Not an officer."

Father Callahan squinted at the man, then lowered his gaze to look at the boy. The boy stared back.

The man had kind eyes framed by heavy wrinkles, a slightly over-sized nose, and salt-and-pepper hair that seemed to be running away from his forehead.

Is this the man I will be living with now? *the boy thought, keeping his gaze locked. The blond man had told him to behave, to make sure that he made eye contact, didn't whine, didn't complain.*

No matter how it went.

"I usually only take girls," the priest said, and the boy's heart sank.

"So I hear," the man replied, the same stern expression on his face. "But this is different — these boys are very special."

Father Callahan looked from the man's right hand, to his left.

"Special?" he said, his eyes locking on the second boy.

The boy resisted the urge to look over at his brother.

"Special."

The priest's substantial brow furrowed.

"How are they special?" he asked.

The blond man let go of the boy's hand and reached into the bag that was slung over his shoulder. He pulled out a plain brown book and held it out to the priest.

"Read this, and you will know."

The priest didn't take it right away. Instead, he eyed the book suspiciously.

"I have to say, this is the strangest visit I've had in a while."

The blond man's face remained expressionless.

"Can you take them?"

The priest chewed his lip, then his eyes darted from the young boy in the man's right hand, to his left.

"I can take one, but not both," he said. "The other one has to go somewhere else."

The blond man's face finally changed. His lips twisted into a frown, but Father Callahan stood his ground and shook his head defiantly.

Even at nine years old, the boy knew that this priest wanted *to take him and his brother in, but he just couldn't do it.*

"One of them," the priest reiterated, even though it pained him to say the words out loud.

The blond man's response was immediate. He pushed his right hand forward, guiding the boy into the threshold of the church. Then he handed him the book.

"Robert, go with Father Callahan. He will find a home for you."

The boy, eyes still downcast, didn't even look at his brother as he obliged.

Robert's eyes snapped open, and like when he had had the dream of the man in the cell, the one who was naked, sitting cross-legged, he felt disoriented and confused.

Blinking rapidly served not only to clear his vision, but to also clear the frostiness that gripped his brain.

Less than a year ago, I was an accountant with a daughter and wife…and now — now this. Dreams, visions, demons that threaten to enter our world.

"I have a brother?" he asked softly, tears streaking down his cheeks. "A twin brother?"

Sean Sommers's lack of emotional response struck Robert as not only insensitive, but it touched a nerve with him.

A nerve that ran deep, and brought with it an unexpected fury.

Robert started to stand, but then lost his balance and fell back to the couch again.

"Why didn't you fucking tell me?"

Shelly reached over and put an arm on his shoulder, but he shrugged it off.

"Why didn't you *fucking* tell me?"

Sean pressed his lips together tightly and shook his head.

"I told you before, Robert, I'm not here to answer all of your questions, as important as they may seem."

This time, Robert bolted upright, making sure to firmly root his feet on the ground.

"Seem? *Seem?* You think that the fact that I...I...I have a twin, that *you*—that somehow *you*—dropped me off at a church, turned my fucking *world* upside down, that I'm—what? Overreacting somehow? Like this shit isn't important?"

Robert reached for the man, but Shelly came between them before he could throttle the smug bastard.

"Like you have no responsibility in this? In *any* of this?" he shouted over her blonde head.

Sean stood then, drink still in hand.

"Oh, I have a role to play," he said softly, eyes downcast. "But that time has yet to come. For now, we have other things to deal with."

"Yeah? Like fucking what? Like Ruth Harlop? George Mansfield? Doctor Andrew Fucking Shaw?"

Sean shook his head.

"Like Carson Ford. And time is running out. We need to act now, or none of your questions will matter at all. If the rift opens, this—" He raised his hands, signifying the massive room in the Harlop Estate, but somehow also indicating something more. "—none of this will matter at all."

Chapter 18

"CAN YOU RESET THE doors? Let me out of here? Smitts is fucking dying out there!"

Peter, his face as pale as a sheet, nodded slowly.

"I can try to reset the entire system, but it means that everything will be offline for at least five minutes, maybe more."

Ben frowned.

"Well, fucking do it, then. I can't do anything from in here. And bring up the camera feed." He pointed at the large monitor, and then the one to the left of it. "I want Carson's room on here, and put wherever Callahan is on this other one."

Peter punched away at the keys, and as Ben requested, Carson's cell was displayed on the center screen.

"What the fuck?"

The warden wiped his eyes, trying to understand what he was seeing.

"The door—show the hallway of Cell Block E."

Peter clacked again, and the hallway appeared on a smaller screen. The door was still closed, and as far as Ben could tell, locked as well.

"The fuck is going on here?" he whispered.

Carson was still sitting cross-legged in his room.

"I could have—I *know* I saw him in the stairwell."

Peter shook his head.

"Door's locked, Chief. Maybe—"

"Restart the system," Ben said firmly. "Do it now."

Peter immediately turned back to his computer screen. A second later, everything went dark again. Only this time, the lights in the room stayed on.

Ben waited, his heart racing.

Was it like Quinn? Is my mind playing tricks on me again? Am I losing my fucking grip?

And then there was Smitts...Smitts fucking bleeding to death just outside the door.

If it wasn't Carson, then who did that to him?

And then there was Father Callahan.

How did he get back here? Why did he come back?

"Fuck," he muttered through gritted teeth, "fuck, fuck, fuck, *fuck*!" If he had had hair atop his bald head, he would have pulled it all out in that moment.

Peter swiveled around.

"You okay?"

Ben waved the man away, then quickly crossed the room to the door and stared down at his long-time friend and one of his most trusted guards. The man had since curled into the fetal position, the blood continuing to leak out from between his hands that were still clutching his stomach. His eyes were fluttering, which Ben took as a good sign.

Stay with me, Smitts. Stay the fuck with me.

He wondered where the other guards were, and then Ben scolded himself for not thinking about his walkie sooner.

They worked on a different system than the other electronics in Seaforth, so they should work.

Please, please work, Ben thought as he pulled the walkie from his belt loop. With a slight hesitation, he turned the dial and pressed the walkie.

"Perry, Lenny, this is Warden Ben Tristen. I need your—"

He let go of the button for a second, and then swore again when all he heard was static.

Maybe the walkies somehow worked on the same system as the rest of the prison. Unlikely, but possible. Or maybe it was the—what did Peter call it—electrical clouds or some shit? Maybe the lightning in the sky had fried them.

"Peter, does the—" *reset affect the talkies,* he was about to ask, when the light on the card reader beside the door beeped.

Ben didn't hesitate. He scanned his card, while his other hand, the one still clutching the walkie, reached for the cross around his neck.

Please...

A second later, the door beeped and the warden of Seaforth Prison pulled it open as quickly as he could manage.

"Smitts!" he yelled as he crouched down beside the man.

Smitts's eyes fluttered, but they didn't open. Ben gently peeled the man's hands away from his stomach, and then cringed at the blood that veritably gushed from an inch-wide wound.

"Fuck! Peter, call Lenny! Get him up here *now!*" Ben covered the wound in Smitts's stomach with his hands. It was hot, and his fingers were immediately soaked with blood. "Stay with me, Smitts. Stay the fuck with me."

Smitts groaned, but said nothing.

"Peter!"

Still squeezing Smitts's stomach, he turned his head back to the door. It had since shut behind him.

"Peter!" he yelled again, his heart rate and his voice escalating.

The door suddenly opened, and Peter peeked out. He opened his mouth to say something, but no words came out.

"What the fuck is going on?"

"Lenny...the guards...the..." His eyes became vacant and he started to swoon. Ben feared that the man was going to faint.

"Peter! Keep it together! What about the guards? About Lenny? What happened?"

The man just stood in the doorway, his mouth agape, his hands hanging limply at his sides.

"*Peter!*"

If it weren't for Smitts lying on the ground before him, Ben would have gone to his IT man and throttled him with his arthritic hands.

Peter's eyes suddenly became clear.

"They're all dead, Ben...every last one of them is dead."

Chapter 19

"I NEVER SIGNED UP for this shit," Shelly whispered.

Robert turned to her, his own eyes wide.

"You didn't? Well I sure as hell didn't either. This is insane. All of it. Sometimes…sometimes I think I was in the car with Wendy the day she died. Sometimes I think that all three of us—me, Wendy, Amy—were all killed in that accident."

"Don't say that."

Robert struggled to keep his anger at bay.

"Why not? I mean, does any of this make sense to you? That I have a twin brother? That I was adopted? That my real father is fucking Leland Black, the Goat, fucking Satan of the underworld?"

Shelly barely managed to keep his eye.

"Oh, lest we forget the fact that somehow you and I and Cal—wherever the fuck he is—are now responsible for keeping this gate closed, for keeping demons out of our world."

Robert grabbed at his temples.

"It's fucked, Shelly—it's royally fucked. And I have no idea what to do."

Shelly moved to him quickly, wrapping her arms around his waist, hugging him tight.

He didn't resist, and instead buried his head in her blonde hair. For a while, nobody said anything.

It was Sean who eventually broke the silence.

"I can't force you to do anything, Robert. All I can do is—as before—ask you to help. But I can't stress how important it is that you do what you can to keep this rift in the Marrow closed. This isn't like Ruth Harlop, and not even like Andrew Shaw, although the latter was closer to the truth, but it's something differently entirely. I need you to come with me and help send Carson to the Marrow—to send him there with Leland, to keep them all there, wrapped up tightly in their own personal hell."

Robert sniffed, wiped the tears from his eyes, and then looked at the man.

How many times have we met since I've been an adult? Three? Four, maybe?

And yet none of those times did the disheveled man before him look the way he did now.

It had been impossible for him to abandon Ruth and Patricia and Dr. Mansfield. How likely was it for him to abandon everyone and everything he cared about in this world?

Robert sighed.

He had made his decision, but he couldn't vouch for Shelly. Robert turned to her, using his fingers to lift her chin.

"You don't have—"

She pushed away.

"Don't do that, Robert," she said sternly. "Don't fucking mansplain this to me. I know I don't have to fucking go with you. But I will. I *will* go with you—I'll help you. I'll help because I I—"

Robert felt his body inadvertently go tense.

Shelly punched him on the shoulder.

"Cause I like going with you, retard. What you think I was going to say?"

Her eyes narrowed.

"Nothing," Robert grumbled, turning away from her glare and bringing his attention back to Sean. "Well, what do we do now?"

The man looked relieved, but the sweat on his brow remained.

"I've got a chopper waiting nearby to take us to the island," Sean said.

Why am I not surprised?

Robert felt like he had before heading to the Seventh Ward, when Cal had had his crowbar and Shelly her bag of toys. And he was armed with nothing. In fact, with the questions that still boiled in his brain, he felt armed with less than nothing.

Cal in his stupid bathrobe and turtleneck, Cal with—

"What about Cal?" he asked suddenly, remembering how his friend had taken off with the kid with the cameras.

Sean's brow furrowed and he shook his head.

"No time—we have to leave now. The rift is growing. Can't you feel it?"

Robert started to shake his head, but Sean interrupted.

"Close your eyes, Robert. Close your eyes and concentrate on what you saw in the Marrow."

Despite not wanting to listen to the man standing across from him, Robert felt compelled to do so. And when he closed his eyes and concentrated, he thought he felt something.

"I think—"

"No, don't think," Sean instructed. Robert felt Shelly hug him again. "Don't think—just let your mind go blank and *feel*."

At first, nothing happened. But as Robert started to breathe more deeply, to center himself with his core, he thought he heard something.

The crash of waves.

"What—?"

"Shhh."

Waves, crashing on the shore. Peaceful, serene.

Perfect.

And then lightning filled the sky.

The sound of thunder.

Of screams, of terror.

Robert's eyes snapped open. His chest had gotten so tight that he thought he was having a heart attack.

"We have to go."

Sean nodded.

"I know, we—"

"No," Robert said sternly. "We have to go *now*."

Chapter 20

WARDEN BEN TRISTEN GRABBED Smitts by the shoulders and dragged him backwards into the control room. Despite his strength, it was still a challenge to maneuver the man's wide, muscular shoulders through the door that pale-faced Peter held open. Breathing heavily, Ben finally cleared the threshold and then fell to the ground with Smitts in his lap.

Peter let the door to close behind them.

"Grab gauze and press it to the wound," Ben instructed, still sitting.

"Gauze? This is a control room, we—"

Ben gently laid Smitts's head on the floor, and then stood, groaning as he stretched his back.

"Grab anything, then, something to keep Smitts from bleeding out, Peter!"

Ben searched the room, purposefully avoiding looking at the monitors. Peter's words still echoed in his head—*the guards, they're all dead*—but he must have just been overreacting. The alternative was unthinkable.

Smitts groaned, and Ben focused on the task at hand.

"There!" he said, pointing at a pile of microfiber cloths piled on a small metal cart near the door. "Grab those and press them on the wound."

Peter did as he was instructed, but Ben noted that as he avoided looking at the monitors, Peter avoided looking at Smitts's bloody midsection.

"Press them hard, Peter."

Peter dropped to a knee, placed the thick pile of blue cloths on the wound, and pressed hard. Smitts's brow furrowed, but his eyes remained closed.

Given the amount of blood outside the door and the smear from when he had been dragged into the room, Ben wasn't sure how long the man would last.

The warden took a deep breath, wiped the sweat from his brow, then finally turned to face the monitors. His heart was racing so fast in his chest that he felt dizzy.

For a split second, Ben felt relief wash over him. His eyes first fell on one of the small monitors, which showed Carson still sitting cross-legged in the center of his cell. He still didn't understand how the man had been in the stairwell just a few minutes ago and was now locked in his cell, but not much this day made sense to him.

His eyes moved to the large monitor next, and a moan escaped his lips.

"No, please, Jesus, *no*."

Ben felt lightheaded, and grabbed the back of Peter's chair to avoid falling to his knees. He closed his eyes tightly, trying to will the scene away. When he opened them again, he was staring through tears.

The mess hall that Smitts and Ben had just finished plowing through their breakfast was displayed front and center. Only now it wasn't empty.

Nearly a dozen men dressed in navy guard uniforms were hanging from the ceiling by nooses made from everything from electric cords to twisted sheets. Their eyes were open, vacant, their tongues hanging from mouths that stood out on their purple faces.

"Oh my god," Ben whispered. "Oh my god." He closed his eyes and shook his head, tears streaming down his cheeks now.

"Please, Lord…how is this possible? How the fuck did this happen?"

Even though the question wasn't intended to be answered, Peter replied nonetheless.

"The inmates…they're out," he said, his voice sounding strangely distant.

Ben gripped the chair back so hard that the leather split. Then, with his thick fingers embedded in the material, he pulled, tearing a huge flap back, revealing thick yellow foam beneath.

"How the *fuck* did this happen?" he growled. He clenched his teeth and resisted the urge to throw the chair through the monitors in front of him. "How the *fuck*…?"

Then, unexpectedly, an image of Father Callahan, his stooped form making a slow path up the long steps to the front of the building, flashed in his mind.

Ben forced himself to look at the monitor again.

He found Perry's thin, dark face among the dead, and there was Lenny, spinning slowly, his back to the camera. Ben's eyes skipped quickly across their faces, trying not to take in any of the horrifying details.

"Father Callahan," he whispered, not finding the old priest hanging in the mess hall. "Where is Father Callahan? And where are the inmates?"

When there was no answer, he turned to face Peter.

The man was still pressing on Smitts's wound, but his eyes were locked on the monitor.

"They're all dead," he whispered. "He promised…they…when…"

Ben wiped more tears from his cheeks, and took a deep breath. All he wanted to do was collapse, curl up into a ball like a child and weep.

But he couldn't do that.

He still had a prison to run. No matter if he and Peter and Smitts, who was dying on the floor by their feet, and Father Callahan, wherever he was, were the only ones left worth saving, he had a job to do.

There were more people to think about than just Seaforth Prison guards. If, somehow, Hargrove hadn't taken the tug and left, if Callahan had convinced him to stay, then there was a boat tied up less than a hundred yards from the front door. And if the inmates managed to get to that…

Ben shook his head.

No, that's not possible.

But he had said the same thing about the power blinking out.

And about the prisoners escaping from their cells.

And about nearly his entire staff being murdered.

And about Carson fucking tearing Quinn's eyes out of his head.

A single tear rolled down Ben's wrinkled cheek, and he quickly wiped it away with the back of his hand. Then he compartmentalized everything he had witnessed this day, burying the horrors in the dark recesses of his mind.

"Where are the inmates?" he asked again after clearing his throat.

When Peter said nothing and just continued to stare, wide-eyed, Ben snapped his fingers in front of the man's face.

Peter shuddered, then seemed to come to. A second later, Smitts groaned, and Peter's eyes rolled in that direction.

Ben snapped again.

"Peter! It's me and you now, we need to keep it together! Where are the inmates? Where are the *fucking* inmates?"

Ben reached for him, intent on shaking some life back into the man. If Peter went dark, all was lost.

He was as good as dead like the others—there was no way he would be able to operate the complicated computer system.

But before he grabbed Peter, the man whipped around and strode toward his now torn chair. He sat, and without another word began clacking away at his keyboard, thankfully shifting the horrific image of the men hanging from the mess hall rafters off screen. Then he began to systematically shift through the different cameras in Seaforth, one at a time.

The first image that appeared was of the row of cells from gen pop, and Ben swallowed hard. The doors to the cells were partway open, their interiors empty.

"Next," he said, his throat suddenly dry.

The following image was of one of the hallways, also empty.

"Next," he repeated.

The next four images were the same; empty, as if the prison had long since been abandoned.

Where the fuck are they?

The next image showed Carson, the little fuck still sitting on the floor in his cell meditating.

In some sick way, Ben was glad that at least Carson wouldn't have the pleasure of killing them himself. If, of course, he had been in his cell the whole time.

Somehow, though, in ways that he didn't understand, Ben knew that Carson was behind this.

All of this.

He didn't rightly believe Father Callahan's ramblings, but he felt, deep down in his guts, that this was all Carson's doing.

"Nex—" he started, but Peter had already switched cameras.

The air was suddenly sucked from Ben's lungs.

"What the fuck are they doing?" he whispered.

Peter didn't answer. Even Smitts, still lying on the floor clutching his bleeding stomach, went quiet, although with his eyes closed he couldn't have seen what was on the screen.

Ben squinted hard.

The inmates, all twenty-two of them, were huddled together, standing outside the door to Cell Block E, their heads hung low, their bodies pressed together. Ben had to concentrate to even pick out the fact that they were actually breathing.

"What are they waiting for?" he whispered after staring at the scene for a full minute. "What are they doing?"

Peter shook his head.

And then there was an audible click, the characteristic sound of the door to Cell Block E opening, and then the screen fizzled with static.

They were waiting to get in.

They were waiting to see Carson.

Movement in one of the side monitors drew Ben's gaze. It was the only monitor that showed an image.

And it was of Carson's cell.

He was smiling, a shit-eating, ear-to-ear grin.

Chapter 21

"YOU'RE JOKING, RIGHT?"

Sean shook his head, while Shelly, who had asked the question, just stared.

Robert, fueled by what he had seen in his mind—the tearing of the Marrow, of the man named Carson sitting on the floor of his cell, his face covered in shadows—didn't have time for questions.

"Shelly, we need to hurry," he shouted over the sound of the helicopter's blades chopping through the night air.

Robert knew little of helicopters, but the bulky black shape was clearly military—this wasn't a chopper that took you for a leisure flight over the Grand Canyon. The nose was thick, heavily armored, and there was a strange lack of markings over the entire exterior.

One call from Sean and the helicopter had landed in under ten minutes on the empty field behind the Harlop Estate. It wasn't just the presence of the helicopter that raised eyebrows, but that Sean had *access* to one. On call, no less.

Robert was reminded of Leland's words, when the man had questioned what he really knew about Sean. About either of them, really.

He still wasn't convinced that Leland was his father, or that he had ever been at the church with the large wooden door, holding hands with Sean, all those years ago. He wasn't even sure if what he had seen of the man in the cell was real.

It could just all be an elaborate trick; Sean could have slipped him some sort of powerful hallucinogen and had primed his mind to these ideas.

But why? To what end? And why him?

Robert shook his head.

But the Marrow, the faces in the flames…Amy's voice…that *had* been real.

Hadn't it?

Shelly eventually overcame her incredulity and mobilized, and Robert followed suit, placing a hand on the small of her back as they followed Sean toward the helicopter. As they neared, the air from the blades blew his jacket wide and whipped his hair back.

Sean reached the helicopter first and he put his foot on the dasher before turning back to them.

"Get in," he shouted, gesticulating wildly with his arms.

Robert helped Shelly into the chopper, and she took a seat across from Sean. He hoisted himself inside and then slid in beside her.

He had never been in a helicopter before, and a strange thought suddenly occurred to him.

Not the circumstances under which I thought I would cross this off my bucket list.

He turned to Shelly, who was deathly pale.

Evidently, riding in a helicopter wasn't her idea of a good time.

Staring at her pretty face, her eyes closed, it dawned on Robert that while he knew little of Sean or Leland, he really didn't know that much about Shelly, either. They had been intimate, of course, but only in the physical sense.

Like Sean, she too was guarded.

If we get out of this, I'm going to start asking more questions. Cal, too, wherever he is. For so long, I've been buried in my own problems. It's about time I started thinking of others, too.

Sean put a set of gray headphones on and instructed them to do the same. Robert helped Shelly unhook hers that hung behind them, and then put his on.

Immediately, the drone of the blades disappeared, and was replaced by an odd and mildly discomforting silence.

And then Sean started to speak, his voice surprisingly clear.

"Mark, take us to the Seaforth."

"Yes, sir."

Sir?

Robert glanced over Sean's shoulder and noticed that there were two men in the cockpit. The one named Mark, the pilot, gripped the controls in gloved hands. Then he pulled back, and Robert's stomach lurched as they lifted off the ground.

Shelly reached over and put an arm across Robert's chest.

He couldn't help smiling, despite the circumstances.

No, this *definitely* wasn't Shelly's idea of a good time.

The other man in the cockpit stared straight ahead, his strong jaw locked. Instead of controls in his hands, his fingers were wrapped around the barrel of a machine gun, the butt embedded into the floor.

Military? Is Sean from the military?

Robert looked over at Shelly, but her eyes were locked out the window as they continue to rise in the air.

"ETA forty-seven minutes. Storm on the island, might make for a bumpy ride."

Shelly visibly swallowed.

Forty-seven minutes…

They were barely forty feet in the air when Sean started speaking, and Robert turned his attention to the man just as the roof of the Harlop Estate, the one that Patricia Harlop had been shoved off, disappeared into the darkness.

"Seaforth Prison currently holds twenty-two inmates, all of whom were deemed too dangerous to house on American soil. That's where the man-made island comes in. The prison has had only one warden since its conception, a man who, by all accounts, is tough and law abiding. Getting long in the tooth, and has mounting health problems, but a good man. There are eleven guards, give or take, mostly ex-military, and an IT man named Peter Granger. All had thorough background checks. The prison runs on a five days on, four days off schedule. Sleeping quarters are located in a small building separate from the prison. Meals get boated in on a weekly basis, and then two cooks—part-timers that work regular hours—are flown in from the mainland to prepare them. There is only one way off the island; a heavily fortified boat that makes a single trip each week."

Robert struggled to take this all in as he continued to swallow to force his lunch from entering his throat. Flying in a helicopter was hardly the romantic experience that he had expected. Still, he was faring better than Shelly, whose head was pressed against the rear cushion, her back ramrod straight, eyes closed.

"And this Warden—"

"Ben Tristen," Sean said, filling in the blank.

"Warden Ben Tristen; he knows we are coming?"

Sean shook his head.

"Lost contact with the prison once the storm started. The system is powered by mainline electricity and generators, with multiple backup power sources and redundancies, and it is *never* supposed to go dark. But it did two days ago. When it came back online, the warden reported that a guard had been murdered. Details are sketchy, and support was supposed to head out to the island. But then the storm hit, and we lost contact again. About the same time you…" Sean let his sentence trail off.

"I what?"

Sean held a finger up and then turned toward the two men in the cockpit behind him.

"Mark, Aiden, set your headphones to channel 3, noise-canceling on."

The pilot nodded, while the other simply reached up and switched a dial on the side of his gray headphones. Aiden's robotic behavior was unsettling to Robert.

Sean turned back to him and Shelly, but Shelly still appeared to be at the mercy of her air sickness and was breathing through pursed lips. He nodded at Robert.

"That was when you started having the dreams."

Now it was Robert's turn to shake his head.

"What do the dreams have to do with this? What the fuck is going on, Sean? What is *really* happening?"

Sean pressed his lips together and paused before answering.

When he finally started to speak, Robert leaned in close and listened.

Chapter 22

FATHER CALLAHAN USED THE keycard that he had taken from Quinn's body and used it to open the front door of the Seaforth Prison. He was thankful that it was just Hargrove that was on the boat, that his old friend Ben had kept the other man, the harder one, the one he called Smitts, by his side. That man was not like Ben and Hargrove; he was not a man of the church.

Hargrove, on the other hand…Father Callahan knew his mother and father from their brief time in South Carolina. Which was probably why the man had agreed to leave him alone with Quinn's body, under the pretext of needing to pray.

And, as he'd predicted, with all that had been going on in the prison, someone had forgotten to take away his pass. Or one of the ridiculous old-fashioned brass keys.

The hardest part had been slipping off the boat undetected. His body was old, worn, and he had nearly fallen into the water when he had climbed over the side. As it was, he had twisted his ankle something fierce, and every step brought with it shooting pains up to his knee.

After watching the tug pull away, Father Callahan crept out from behind the bushes and struggled mightily against the pouring rain and strong winds, and soon he once again found himself back inside the prison. As he crossed the threshold, the outer door closed and locked automatically, finally offering him a reprieve from the elements.

With a deep, racking breath that brought with it a series of dry coughs, the priest found himself alone in the small holding room.

He teased the key out of his robes and put it in the lock and turned it, the metal biting deep into his gnarled fingers.

Then he grabbed the door and pulled.

Nothing happened; it wouldn't open.

He fiddled with the lock again, but when he tried the door second door, his efforts were met with the same result.

Then he remembered Ben using his walkie to signal to someone who opened the door remotely.

Father Callahan scolded himself for being so stupid. He was just a frail, old man—how was he supposed to break into a prison so secret that only a handful of people had even heard of it?

But he had to try. He had no choice but to try.

Two nights ago, he had had a vision—a vision of a rift in the Marrow, and it all started here. He didn't know if it was just a coincidence that Ben had called him, or if he too had picked up signals from the Marrow and just didn't know it.

But the details didn't matter. And it didn't matter how close he was with Ben, how far back their friendship ran.

Father Callahan had to get inside—he *had* to talk to Carson. And he had to stop the man, no matter what the cost.

Ben had been too soft on the man, and as the quiddity in the prison increased, the strength that Carson possessed grew with it.

Despite the vision, Father Callahan had thought he had more time. His first intention had been to just visit the prison, check out the scene, and then seek out one of the Guardians.

But after seeing the video of Carson with the eyeballs clutched in his hands, and the poor guard speaking of the Goat, he knew that time was of the essence. And the *feeling*, the tightness in his chest that he felt even now, made it abundantly clear that there was no time to seek the others.

He himself was not a Guardian, just the keeper of the book. And what was happening at Seaforth followed closely the prophecy in *Inter vivos et mortuos*.

The prophecy that described a sadistic murderer opening the gateway to the Marrow, allowing the evil to spill into this world, and forever poisoning the Marrow Sea.

It was up to him to stop Carson. There was no time to reach out to the others.

Father Callahan took a deep breath, feeling his lungs constrict, and he fought the urge to cough again.

Then he stepped back, and for some reason he flicked a hand up at the camera in a half-hearted wave.

A second later, the lights clicked out and the inner door swung open.

Chapter 23

"...WHAT'S REALLY GOING ON here?" Robert asked.

"Truth is, I'm not sure anymore. All I know is that a few years back, there was a disturbance of sorts, a tremor, if you will, something that I haven't felt in...well, I have *never* felt like this before."

Robert eyed the man suspiciously, remembering Leland's words.

How much do you really know about Sean Sommers? Do you look at him with the same disdain in your eyes as you do me?

"You *felt* it?"

Sean nodded.

"Like you, I can feel things—only difference is I've been at this a lot longer than you have."

Robert made a face.

"Who are you? And, more importantly, who am *I*?"

For a long time, Sean just stared at him. He had recovered somewhat from his disheveled appearance at the Harlop Estate a few hours ago; his tie was still hanging loosely around his neck, his hair messy, but at least his face was no longer slack. Something about his hardened expression, despite having incited rage back at the estate, was oddly comforting under these circumstances.

Familiar, even.

"I told you that I'm not here to answer your questions, Robert," he said at last. "That's not my role to play in all of this."

Robert immediately opened his mouth to protest, but Sean held up a hand to silence him.

"But given what has happened—what *is* happening—I feel obliged to tell you more. Because I fear that...well, you were destined to find out eventually anyway. It's probably best if you heard from me, and not from *him*." The man's ramblings sounded to Robert as if he were trying to convince himself, rather than the other way around. He held up a finger again before continuing. "Aiden? Mark? ETA?"

They waited in silence for a moment, and when there was no reply, Sean nodded and indicated Shelly with his hand.

"What about her?"

Sean gestured for him to slip the headphones off her head. Robert turned to face his lover; her breathing was rhythmic, her expression slack.

She was sleeping.

A bout of guilt hit him as he reached over and gently teased the headphones from her ears, remembering what she had said about being honest with her. Her eyelids fluttered slightly with the reintroduction of the sound of the storm and the helicopter blades, but she remained asleep.

Shelly demanded that he was honest, but this was different.

Robert had the sneaking suspicion that just hearing what Sean was about to say would put her in danger.

As he hung the headphones on the hook beside her head, he couldn't help but feel that it was a mistake bringing her along with him—with *them*.

Deep down, he was grateful that Cal had run off, that he wouldn't be exposed to whatever was going to happen in the prison. Because if the sensation he had experienced during his vision was anything like what was really happening there, then it was better off to remain ignorant.

"Robert?" Sean's voice asked quietly in his headphones, and Robert regained his focus. He lifted his gaze to meet Sean's eyes, and the man leaned forward intently. And then he started to speak.

"I'm going to tell you what I know, Robert. It isn't everything, and the truth is that there are those out there that know more than I do—much more. All I ask is that you keep an open mind. Can you do that?"

Robert nodded, and Sean continued.

"I guess there is no better place to start than with Carl Jung."

"Carl Jung?" Robert asked, incredulous. "*The* Carl Jung?"

Sean pressed his lips together, clearly annoyed by the interruption.

"Yes, that Carl Jung. Are you familiar with his thesis on the collective unconscious?"

Robert shrugged.

"Not really; I mean, I've heard of him, like I've heard of Freud, but I don't know much about any of his work. After all, I'm an accountant, not—"

"Jung believed that in addition to the individual self, the persona, there exists a collective unconscious, an archetypal representation of our most base desires. Sex, lust, anger, love, madness. As humans, these exist outside of our *selves*, and we draw from them. Through individuation, we become less reliant on this unconsciousness, less able to access it. But for some of us...for a certain type of person..." Sean let his sentence trail off, and Robert took the opportunity to jump in.

"For the James Harlops, the Andrew Shaws."

Sean nodded.

"The Carson Fords of this world, they grab on to the most heinous of these archetypes of the collective unconscious and hold on tight. You see, Carl was wrong about one thing. The collective unconscious doesn't exist in the cloud."

"It exists in a Sea. The Marrow Sea," Robert whispered.

"That's right—although it has been called many different things over the years. In any event, it is from within this sand and sea that most of human consciousness ends up, and it is from these seeds that new quiddity are born."

A frown started to form on Robert's lips as he tried to understand.

"You mean like reincarnation?"

"No, not exactly. It's more like an amalgamation of past lives, mixed together to create a unique individual. It's like our DNA, in a sense; the building blocks are the same for twins, let's say, but for a variety of reasons they are different, all unique. In part because of individuation."

"But if what you're describing is the sea and the sand, what about the fire? The faces?"

Sean cleared his throat.

"Despite having many names, I've always been in favor of 'The Marrow.' Loosely, the Marrow means 'the middle,' which is where you were. Standing on the shore, you made it to the place only a handful of people have ever been before and returned. The collective unconscious was lapping at your toes, but above…above was the embodiment of pure evil. You see, evil can't exist in the Marrow Sea—the most ruthless of acts, murder, rape, slavery, are centered in the *self*. And this, my friend, is the Hell that you saw."

Robert exhaled loudly.

"Why? Why me?" he asked.

Sean shrugged, and averted his gaze.

"That's complicated, Robert. And, quite truthfully, I don't know the exact reason."

Robert didn't press; he could tell that Sean was more than a little uncomfortable sharing what he already had, and there were still many other questions that he wanted to ask.

"I've never...I mean, how do you know about this? About any of this?"

Sean's eyes returned to Robert's.

"From a book—*Inter vivos et mortuos; Between the living and the dead.*"

He paused after saying the words, either because it pained him to do so or because he expected the Latin-sounding name to come as some sort of revelation.

If he was expecting the latter, he was sorely mistaken. Robert just stared at the man, dumbfounded.

Eventually, Sean continued.

"No one knows who wrote it, or where it came from. It's a simple leather-bound book written in basic Latin. Abrupt, to the point—almost Hemingway-esque in style. No wasted words. And in it, it describes the most basic of human conflicts: the desire for self-immolation or self-preservation. And this is the decision that every human quiddity must face when they land on the shores of the Marrow, or at least that's what the book states—we can't be certain, because, well, until recently, no one has ever made it back. On the shores, you can give yourself to the Marrow Sea, replenish the stock of quiddity for others that have yet to be born, or you can stay whole, retain your identity, but in doing so you are banished to the flames above. You've seen the faces—you know what I mean."

An image of the fiery sky with the horrible, screaming mouths flashed in Robert's mind, and a shudder passed through him.

"Yeah, I've seen them," he croaked.

"The book also describes a group of Guardians, people empowered with making sure that things stay in order. Leland was one of the Guardians, as am I—and there are others, too. Fewer now than there were, but still a fair number."

"Was Carl Jung one of these guardians?"

Sean shrugged.

"Maybe, don't know for sure. But based on his writings, I would think it highly likely. Either that or he was very close with one."

"But if Leland was a Guardian, why is he trying to create a rift?"

Sean sighed, a heavy, exasperated sigh that seemed to make his entire face slacken.

"*Something* happened, something that changed him, and instead of wanting to keep order, to maintain a balance between the Fire and the Sea, the self and the collective unconscious, Leland began working for the opposite. He became obsessed with the Self, tried to convince all of the Guardians that they were misled, that the Sea was actually Hell, and that not only should everyone choose the flames, but that they can *come back*. Most of the other Guardians thought that he had lost his mind, but some thought differently. You see, *Inter vivos et mortuos* speaks of a prophecy, of a time when a man rises up and opens the floodgates, letting the quiddity flow *backwards*. And since all the good has already been sacrificed, all that's left is—"

"The faces in the flames."

"Yes," Sean said simply. "And the walls are weakening. Every time someone's quiddity stays too long here on earth, every time their decision is delayed, the barrier between this world and theirs gets thinner, and he gets stronger."

Robert's brow furrowed.

"So what happened to Leland? Why is he on the shores? Why is he...did he die?"

This time, Sean didn't answer.

"Sean? What happened to Leland? How did he get to the Marrow?"

Still nothing.

Robert leaned forward and reached for the man across from him. Sean immediately recoiled, and aimed a finger at Robert's face.

"Don't touch me," he warned, his voice returning to the hardened rasp of which Robert was more familiar. "Leland has branded you, and if you touch me he will be able to find me. That can't happen."

Robert leaned away, taken aback by the man's sudden change in mood. This time, he refused to let it go.

"What do you mean? Fuck, Sean, what happened to him?"

Sean pressed his lips together tightly and then turned his gaze to Shelly.

She was waking, a look of confusion on her face.

"That's it, no more stories. We have work to do."

Shelly groaned and stretched her arms, and Robert, deep in thought, reluctantly lowered his eyes to out the helicopter window. The skies had darkened significantly, and a chill passed through him.

Robert could see water below.

Just as Shelly started to put her headphones back on, confused as to why they had come off her head in the first place, Robert's own erupted in a burst of static.

"Sir, we are approaching the storm I warned you about. ETA ten minutes to Seaforth, but it's going to be a very bumpy ride from here on out. Sit tight, everyone."

Robert swallowed hard, and tried to bring up Leland's face, the one he had glimpsed for just a fraction of a second before he had been transported back to the land of the living.

Nothing came, which was only fitting, because after the story that Sean had told him, he felt completely empty.

What do you really know about Sean Sommers?

Chapter 24

"WE STILL HAVE GUN storage up here?" Ben asked as he continued to apply pressure to Smitts's stomach. The bleeding had slowed somewhat, and the man had regained some semblance of consciousness. Not enough yet to actually speak, but the warden hoped that he would soon be able to tell him what had happened just outside the door. "Peter?"

Ben raised his eyes.

Peter was still sitting in his chair, his eyes locked on the monitor that showed the inmates huddled outside Cell Block E.

"What the fuck are they doing?" he whispered just loudly enough for Ben to hear. "The door is unlocked. Why aren't they going in?"

"Peter! Wake the fuck up! Snap out of it!"

Ben saw the back of the man's head visibly shake, and then he slowly turned, his narrow features pale, his jaw slack.

"What, Chief?"

"Is the gun storage up here?"

"Yeah, over there," Peter answered, pointing his chin toward the corner of the room. Ben followed his directions, but saw nothing other than more computers and cables. It had been a while since he had been up in the Tower, he realized, as he had stayed away mostly because all of this computer shit made him uncomfortable.

Instinctively, his hand went to the cross around his neck.

That, on the other hand, gave him comfort. Or it had—now it just made him nervous for Father Callahan, who they couldn't seem to find anywhere on any of the cameras.

Did he really see Quinn, too?

For a moment, he wished he had spent more time with Father Callahan, that he had listened to his old friend speak for longer.

There was something going on here that was beyond his pay grade.

And likely his skillset as well.

"Where?"

"Right there," Peter replied.

"Goddammit, Peter! *Where?* Get the fuck out of your chair and open it for me!"

Peter rose from his chair with such speed that it wheeled away from him, forcing Ben to hold his hand up so it didn't bump into him and Smitts. The gangly man made his way quickly across the circular room and to a cabinet that at first blush looked like a computer housing. But when he scanned his keycard at the reader, it went red.

"No access," he said simply.

Ben frowned.

He was beginning to fear that Peter was losing it...or had lost it already.

"Use mine," Ben instructed, tossing his card to the man. It struck him in the chest and fell to the floor. Peter quickly bent and picked it up. When he scanned the warden's card, the lock disengaged and the door swung open, revealing two shotguns and two handguns. There was also a stack of rounds at the bottom of the locker and a stun gun.

Ben breathed a sigh of relief.

Peter had been trying to call out of the prison as soon as they'd realized that the inmates had escaped, but they had had no luck. Cell phones, VoIP, email, nothing seemed to be able to leave the island. And the thought of being up here in the Tower with the power to the doors blinking in and out and *them* down there, doing whatever the fuck they were doing, with no weapons other than the small pistol on his hip, was enough to make the hardened Warden Ben Tristen feel naked.

But now, with the shotguns, they might stand a chance. They could at least hold out up here until the storm passed and help arrived. Those nutjobs could stay huddled like retarded lemmings all they wanted. With all of the other guards dead...

He felt a pang in his stomach.

On my watch...and Father Callahan is still out there—but he came back, he was supposed to leave, goddammit.

Ben knew that waiting them out was the best course of action, maybe their only course of action, but he still couldn't help feel the nagging pull of vengeance on the corners of his soul.

They should pay for what they did to my men...to my friends. And Father...I can't let anything happen to him.

He glanced up at Peter, who was staring at the guns with reverence and awe. Then he turned his attention back to Smitts on the ground beneath him.

If Quinn was here, and Smitts was still able to move...then we might have been able to take them.

"Boss?" his friend suddenly said with a grunt. He shifted his weight, but Ben held him down.

"Yeah? Best you lay still, Smitty. You lost a lot of blood."

The man shook his head.

"...need to sit up."

"Smitts, sit—"

Smitts gritted his teeth defiantly.

"Up," he demanded, and Ben had no choice but to allow the man to scooch onto his elbows. At the same time, he pushed Ben's hands away from his midsection and pressed the gauze to his own wound.

His breathing increased, but after a moment it stabilized.

Ben was surprised that the man was even conscious, let alone speaking and sitting up. He knew Smitts was tough, but the warden was worried that this might be the man's last hoorah.

His final wind.

And then it would just be him and Peter.

"I—" He cleared his throat. "I saw Quinn."

Ben sprang to his feet.

"W-w-what?" he stammered. "What do you mean you saw *Quinn*?"

Smitts nodded, but then threw his head back in agony, his hands tensing on his stomach. The dark navy Seaforth Prison uniform was nearly black on Smitts's stomach and chest.

"I saw him," Smitts repeated through gritted teeth. His eyes were closed now, his hard chin aimed at the ceiling. "He was holding his face, and blood was dripping from his hands. Fuck, Ben, I know this is crazy, but I *saw* him."

Ben gaped at his long-time friend. And then he said the only thing he could think of.

Almost ashamedly, he whispered, "I saw him too."

Smitts didn't seem at all surprised by this; maybe it was the pain or the blood loss, or maybe he just *knew*, but Smitts barely reacted.

Ben took a deep breath.

"What happened to you, Smitts?" he asked, dreading the answer.

"He…he stabbed me, Ben. Quinn fucking stabbed me."

Ben shook his head.

"What the fuck is going on at Seaforth?" he asked, fighting back tears again.

Someone answered, but it wasn't Smitts.

It was Peter, and when the warden raised his gaze to look at the man, his eyes went wide.

There was a shotgun leveled at his head.

"Carson's setting them free, Chief. He's setting us all free."

Chapter 25

"WE GO IN HOT," SEAN shouted over the rain that pelted the helicopter. "Aiden, you take the lead. Mark, get the bird back into the air, get away from the storm, but don't stray too far. We're going—"

A bolt of lightning split the pitch-black sky, and the helicopter swayed to the left. Robert felt his stomach lurch along with the tilting of the helicopter.

"—put us down, Mark! Get us down wherever you can!"

The helicopter dipped again, and Robert nearly fell into Shelly's lap. She cried out, but then he managed to right himself. As they got closer to the building, a gray cement structure that, aside from a single turret, was a nearly perfect square, the structure started to shield them from the worst of the elements.

"Sean!" Robert shouted into his mouthpiece after adjusting the headphones that had been knocked askew. "What the fuck are *we* supposed to do?"

The man's answer was immediate.

"You and Shelly stay behind me. Even if the power is down, Aiden will find a way in. He goes first, me next, then you two. I need you to keep your eyes and ears open. If you see any inmates or quiddity, let me know."

Robert raised an eyebrow.

"But what am I here for? Why do you need me? Why don't you just send Aiden in there and blast the shit out of the place?"

Sean shook his head.

"It's too late for that. Remember your dream? The rift has already started to open. I need you to close it."

The helicopter dipped again, and Shelly gasped. Robert reached over and tried to put his arm around her, but she pushed him away.

"I can handle it, Rob," she told him.

Robert turned back to Sean, who had lifted part of the bench beside him and pulled out two dark rain jackets. For a split second before the bench slammed closed again, Robert thought he caught sight of another box inside, a smooth gray shape.

"Put these on," he instructed as he tossed them over. Robert caught both and handed one to Shelly.

"Close the rift? *How?*" Robert yelled back as he slipped the jacket over his head. He had to pull the headphones off first, and when he did, a strong gust of wind rocked the helicopter.

For a sickening second when the headphones flew from his hand, nearly striking Shelly before smashing against the glass, Robert was convinced that they were going to plummet to their deaths.

And the only thing that flashed in his mind was the image of Amy.

How could I hear her voice if she became part of the Sea? Shouldn't she be gone by now?

"Hold on!"

Without his headphones, the pilot's shouts were barely audible over the storm.

They dipped again, and this time Shelly reached out and held him tight. Even Sean looked pale, his hands gripping the sides of his seat. During Robert's swaying, the man had also put a rain jacket on.

Lightning split the sky high above them again, and a second later, the copter landed with a jolt on the ground.

Robert immediately unclicked his seatbelt and moved toward the door, but Sean shook his head.

"Aiden first, then me, then you."

Robert nodded, thankful that the man with the Uzi or sub-machine gun or whatever the hell it was was going to enter the prison full of psychopaths first. As he watched the man exit the cockpit, sliding onto the ground and down to one knee like butter out of a warm pan, gun poised out in front of him, Shelly leaned over to him and whispered something in his ear.

Startled, he nearly pitched forward, and he didn't pick up what she said.

"What?" he yelled over his shoulder at her. Despite being on the ground, the copter blades somehow seemed even louder here. When there was no immediate answer forthcoming, he looked at her. Shelly's eyes were wide, and he could have sworn that there were tears in them.

"Shel? You—"

But the door to the copter was yanked open from the outside, and the roaring wind and rain swallowed his words. Out of his periphery, he saw Sean rise to his feet and jump out of the helicopter, just as Shelly whispered something that looked to Robert like '*snow.*'

Snow?

Rain pelted him on the back, and although the air was frigid, there was no snow on the horizon for another six months, probably more.

What the hell is she talking about?

"What?" he shouted again, but it was Sean who responded.

"Out, Robert, we're in the open here!"

Robert turned back and the immediacy on Sean's face spurred him to action.

He made a mental note to ask Shelly what the hell she was talking about later.

The rain struck him in the face, and he squinted hard. Although Sean was ushering him toward Aiden, who was still on one knee, gun aimed at the concrete structure that Robert could barely make out in the torrential downpour, he waited by the open door, helping Shelly out.

This time she accepted his aid.

And then, with one arm wrapped around her waist, they started to run.

Behind them, Robert heard the pitch of the helicopter blades increase; he didn't need to look back to know that it was airborne.

In a few moments, it would be like it had never been here at all.

Chapter 26

"Peter? What the fuck are you doing? *Peter*, put the fucking gun down."

Peter's face seemed to have changed from a few seconds ago. Instead of looking pale and scared, the man had a sinister smile and his eyes…there was something wrong with his eyes.

They were dark, bordering on black. It was as if the pinprick pupils that Ben had observed upon entering the control room had grown large enough to take over the entire globes.

"How 'bout I blast you in the face instead, Chief?"

The warden started to stand, but Peter took a menacing step forward, pushing the butt of the shotgun deeper into his shoulder. Ben had seen enough men do this in preparation for the expected kickback to know that he was serious.

Swallowing hard, he raised his arthritic hands and crouched back onto his haunches.

"Alright, alright, I'm staying here, okay? Why don't you just tell me what the hell is going on?"

Peter eased the pressure of the shotgun on his shoulder and Ben felt his heart rate slow a little.

But his mind was still racing.

What the fuck is wrong with him?

"You want to know why Quinn went into Carson's room?"

Smitts craned his neck around with a groan at the mention of Quinn's name, and Peter quickly swung the gun around to him.

"And you sit the fuck down, Smitts, or I'll put another hole in your body."

"Peter, what the fuck are you doing?"

The man's wild, dark eyes flicked back to the warden.

"I'll ask the questions here, Chief. And I asked whether you want to know what happened to your friend Quinn—if you wanted to know why he went in Carson's cell."

Ben stared at the man, while at the same time scanning the room with his peripheral vision. He had no idea what had gotten into Peter, but he didn't rightly care—at least not right now. In this moment, his goal was to subdue the man and get help for Smitts. Third was to keep the prisoners locked in the prison. This fucking computer dipshit's motives were far down his list.

"Why'd he do it, Peter?" Ben asked.

He couldn't go for his gun on his hip. Although the man before him spent most of the time in front of the computer, he knew how to use a gun. Even the two part-time cooks knew how to use all of the guns inside the prison. That wasn't to say that they had access, of course—Peter's card being rejected at the gun cabinet was testament to that—but they knew how to use them.

So, no, he couldn't reach for his gun unless he wanted his face to be peppered with buckshot. The only other weapons he had on his person were the standard-issue Taser and his telescoping nightstick, neither of which would do any damage at this range.

The only advantage he had was that there were two of *them* and one of *him*. Even incapacitated as he was, Smitts was conscious.

The hard, dying bastard might be capable of one last, heroic act.

"Peter? Why did Quinn go see Carson?"

Resisting the urge to steal a glance down at his fallen comrade, he instead grimaced as if his knee was aching, and then shifted a foot or so closer to the hands at Smitts's stomach.

"Carson isn't who you think he is," Peter said calmly. "He may have once been a psychopath, especially when he was with Buddy, but not now. Now he is *enlightened.* Do you know what it's like? Huh? Staring at others for so long that you lose your *self?* I sit up here, locked away, watching, waiting. But then...but that was before Carson. Carson saved me...he started to talk to me, he promised me that he would help find who I *really am.*"

Peter paused as if to mull this over, his eyes becoming vacant. Ben wondered if this was his chance, if the man was zoned out enough that might be able to pounce...or go for his weapon...or...

Or reach for my cross.

Peter's eyes became clear again, saving Ben from making a decision that would surely have resulted in bloodshed.

And Seaforth had seen enough dying and death for one day.

"Do you ever think about dying, Ben?"

Ben eyed the shotgun.

"I've got a fucking shotgun in my face. So, yeah. I've thought about it."

Peter snickered.

"I mean at other times."

Ben shrugged.

"Ah, shit, you must be what? Pushing seventy now?"

"Seventy-two," Ben corrected the man.

"Damn, you look good for seventy-two. Anyways, you must have thought about your own death, then. It's only natural."

Peter waited, and Ben couldn't help but think back to when his wife, Angie, had passed more than two decades ago from breast cancer.

She had looked so horrible in the end: bald, skin so thin it looked like stretched cellophane. She was barely able to talk after the chemo had ruined her voice box.

Yeah, he had thought about dying. He had thought about it a lot.

Peter nudged his chin at the cross that hung out from Ben's shirt.

"Yeah, I bet you have. Well let me tell you, that shit that you believe in? That cross? Jesus 'n' all that? Well, sorry to break it to you, but that's all garbage. There is no heaven, no hell. There is only the Marrow."

"The *what*?" Ben asked, unable to keep the incredulity from creeping into his voice.

Again, Peter chuckled.

"The Marrow is like a communist or Marxist version of Hell, my friend. And Carson is going to change all that."

"You've lost your mind, Peter. Put the gun down and let's talk this out. There are twenty-two crazed murderers down there that are just itching to tear us apart. You want that? You want them to leave this place, go back to the city? Is that what you want? Is that what Carson's gonna do? Because let me tell you, it ain't gonna happen."

Peter shrugged.

"Doesn't matter. What matters is that once we leave this place, we can keep *who we are*. You want that, don't you?"

"Peter, what the fuck are you talking about? You been cruising the damn conspiracy websites again?"

"No, no websites."

"Well then who the hell poisoned your mind with all this shit? It's just the stress. I get it, you're an IT guy, weren't cut out for this. Well, let me tell you something. It has fucked me up too. Just put the gun down."

"Leland," the man whispered.

"What?"

"Leland told me about the Marrow."

Ben's mind was spinning now. None of this made sense. But while Peter's words seemed like the ramblings of a madman, it also sounded somehow familiar.

As if he had heard something similar before. He shook his head, trying to clear it.

It didn't work.

"Who the hell is Leland?"

"Don't you see, Chief? Leland is the one behind it all, he's the one that is guiding Carson. But they can't do it alone. He needs Father Callahan to open the rift, which is why I let him back in."

An image of the old man in the dark robes flashed in Ben's mind. With all that had happened, he had completely forgotten about his priest—his friend. And he was reminded of the words that Father Callahan had uttered back in the chapel and how they had sounded eerily similar to what Peter had said just now.

I have to talk to Carson.

Ben's heart started racing and his eyes inadvertently flicked to the bay of monitors, while at the same time he felt a gentle tug at his belt.

"No," he whispered. "Please tell me you didn't let him back in."

"Oh, oh yes I did, Chief. I let him in because Carson needs him. He needs him to open the door. He needs—"

What happened next confirmed Ben's notion that Smitts had one final act to play in this menagerie of death. And he acted so quickly that Peter didn't even get a chance to squeeze a shot off.

Smitts, who had been tugging at the warden's belt for several minutes now, gave a stiff yank and pulled Ben's Taser free. Then, in one smooth movement, the man pressed the button, activating a crackle followed by a brilliant white arc between the leads. But instead of moving toward Peter, Smitts kept moving his arm over his own body before jamming the electrical current into a large series of cables that ran across the floor to the junction box on the opposite wall.

A second before the lights blinked out for a third time, Ben caught sight of his friend's body convulsing, blood spraying from his mouth and from his stomach where Quinn's spirit had stabbed him.

And then the deafening sound of the shotgun going off filled the control room.

Chapter 27

FATHER CALLAHAN TOOK ANOTHER step, gliding deeper into the halls of Seaforth Prison.

He wasn't one of the Guardians, one of the nineteen—of which there were only five left, if you counted that bastard Leland—but the keeper of the book. Still, he knew what was at stake.

After all, he had the *Inter vivos et mortuos*. He had even learned Latin to translate it.

He knew what was at stake.

Father Callahan moved slowly, his old, ruined body barely shuffling along now; the pain that was previously contained to his ankle now seemed to envelop his entire body.

He had to find Carson. *Needed* to find him before the rift was opened.

Inter vivos et mortuos, or the Marrow, needed to remain intact.

Ben Tristen was his friend, his good friend, and a loyal follower of the faith. But he was naive.

Father Callahan slipped a hand beneath his robe and his gnarled hand closed around the grip of the knife buried within.

Ben hadn't searched him when he had entered the prison.

Carson *had* to be stopped, even if it meant doing the same horrible thing that they had done to Leland all those years ago.

The Marrow needed to remain intact.

Their worlds needed to remain separate.

The *Inter vivos et murtuos* had written of such a day, and Father Callahan would do everything in his power to stop *that* day from being *today*.

Even if it meant dying.

The old man coughed into his elbow.

Even if it meant killing.

And then, as he lifted his foot to take another step, he was suddenly shrouded in darkness as the lights above flicked out.

Despite everything he knew about the true nature of life and death, Father Callahan started whispering *Our Father*.

Chapter 28

"TRY THE CARD I gave you," Sean yelled to Aiden.

The man looked back at him and shook his head. Robert, huddled against the downpour, watched the odd interaction between the two men. It was clear that Sean was in charge, that much had been obvious from their time in the chopper, but now it seemed that they had reached a standstill.

"You open it, sir," Aiden replied curtly. It was evident that this man had one role and one role only: to make sure that Sean and Shelly and Robert remained safe, remained alive.

He would not put his assault rifle down to open a door and jeopardize them all.

No matter who ordered him.

This realization offered Robert comfort, despite the fact that he still wasn't sure what he was doing here.

His job would be to close the rift— but *how*?

He was brought back to the time when he had first met Shelly back at the Harlop Estate, a time that seemed years ago.

Bind the spirits.

But *how*?

Blind luck had gotten him out of that situation. He just hoped that it hadn't run out here at Seaforth.

Shelly nudged him forward, and Robert gave her a look.

"Go on," she said.

Robert frowned.

Fuck, looks like I'm taking orders, too.

He took a giant step forward, and watched as the man with the rifle gave him a onceover.

Robert did the same, and for the first time he got a good look at the man that was in charge of protecting them all.

Aiden was square-jawed, but not in the same way as Sean; his jaw was more pronounced and covered in a five-o'clock shadow. He was the type of guy that always had the same amount of hair on his face, no matter how long ago they shaved. Sometime during the flight, he had jammed a wad of dip into his bottom lip, causing it to jut forward. There was a scar that ran vertically through his left eyebrow, which cradled dark, penetrating eyes. His hair, which appeared short beneath a plain, black do-rag, was dark like the stubble on his face. The man's forearms, which jutted out from beneath a three-quarter-length tight shirt, were like rebar—tough, corded, muscular.

It took Robert a moment to realize that the man was holding a pass out to him.

As he stepped forward and took it from Aiden—who held it for a second too long, he noted—Robert stared into his eyes.

They were dark and small, but they weren't cold like Sean's. The man was serious. He had a job to do, an important one, but he wasn't unfeeling, uncaring.

Aiden indicated the small black box beside the thick metal door. Robert nodded and moved past the man, noting that he adjusted his position so that the automatic weapon was now aimed over his shoulder.

As Robert moved toward the door, he was suddenly struck with a sense of déjà vu.

He was back in the Seventh Ward again, using the card to exit, and to chase after the hideous creature called George.

But back then he didn't have a fully automatic assault rifle at his back and twenty-two of America's worst killers in the building before him.

The building he was poised to unlock.

"Robert, the door," he heard Sean say from behind him, snapping him out of his reverie. Reaching out, he swiped the card through the reader.

It beeped and went red.

"Try again," Sean instructed.

Robert did, but the result was the same.

"Motherfuckers. Supposed to be a skeleton key—and the fucking thing worked earlier."

Earlier? Sean was here earlier?

"Try again, Robert."

For the third time, the keycard reader remained red after he swiped the card.

"Sir? You want me to get Mark back here? Got some C4 in the cab."

Sean waved him off.

"No, not yet. There's another way in: the chapel."

Aiden's scarred eyebrow raised.

"Sir?"

Sean nodded.

"The cha—"

But the lights on the outside of the prison suddenly went dark, cutting his words short.

"Try it now, Robert."

Robert hesitated, confused by what had just happened. At the same time, Aiden switched the light on his rifle on, bathing the metal door in bright light.

"Now, Robert—forget the card, try the door!"

Robert grabbed the door handle and pulled it. He had expected it to remain locked, so when he pulled and the door actually opened, he stumbled backwards. If it weren't for Aiden's large hand on his back, he would have fallen to the mud.

The man also somehow stepped around him at the same time, his fingers grabbing the crack between the door and the frame that Robert had opened. He pulled it wide, and held it open with his foot, while systematically scanning the interior of the room.

Yeah, this was definitely the man that Robert wanted protecting them.

"Clear," Aiden said before ushering them inside.

It wasn't until they were all inside what appeared to Robert to be a small holding cell that he realized Sean was holding a pistol in his right hand. It was pathetic compared to what Aiden held out in front of them, but he once again felt naked.

Like he had in the Seventh Ward.

No crowbar for him.

No blowtorch.

No Cal, either.

"Fuck," he muttered, and Shelly shot him a confused look.

He was an accountant, not a fucking soldier.

Not a ghostbuster.

Not anything, really.

Just a family man that missed his daughter.

Missed normal life.

"Fuck," he said again, this time a little louder.

Sean reached out and grabbed the inner door. Unlike the outer door, this one didn't appear to be electronic. Thankfully, the old-fashioned lock was hanging, as if someone had entered not long ago and had left it open for some unknown reason. The door opened without resistance, and Sean motioned for Aiden to step in front again.

"Let's shut this fucker Carson down before he opens the gateway," Sean said, a strange expression on his face. "Let's shut it all down, Robert. Once and for all."

Part III – Guardians of the Marrow

Chapter 29

THE SHOTGUN BLAST ERUPTED like a small explosion in the control room, blinding and deafening all three occupants. Ben felt a gust of warm air hit him in the face, followed by a stinging sensation in his left cheek.

But it didn't matter.

Being blinded and in pain didn't slow him down. Old or not, he trained for this. He built his body every day for this exact moment. He just never thought it would be to subdue one of his own.

Ben Tristen lunged at the spot where the blast had come from. Despite the ringing in his ears, he heard the sound of Peter calling out, muffled, as if shouted under water, and then his shoulder collided with the skinny man's midsection. For the second time in a matter of seconds, he felt hot air on his head and face, only this time it was the air being forced out of Peter's lungs.

Peter grunted as Ben continued through the shoulder tackle, driving them both backward. Two agonizing steps later, there was a crunch as Peter's back collided with something solid. And yet Ben kept shoving with his legs, grinding his shoulder into the man's solar plexus.

Peter tried to bring his arms, and maybe the gun, down on top of Ben's head, but his body was folded and he couldn't rear back and put any strength into his blows.

When the flailing slowed and the gasping for air reached a fever pitch, Ben relaxed his quads slightly. When he felt Peter draw in a fresh breath, he drove the top of his head upward.

Ben was a big man with a big, bald head, and when it connected with the underside of Peter's chin, his jaws immediately smashed together. Blood or spit, or maybe both, sprayed the top of his head as Peter's face was launched skyward. When it rebounded back and he felt the rest of the man's body go limp, Ben knew Peter was out cold.

Only then did he allow himself to breathe. And then, almost immediately, his body started to ache. Ben slid to one side, flipping over and into a seated position, while at the same lowering Peter's body to the ground.

Gently.

Maybe *too* gently.

He sat there for a second, his eyes closed, his lungs, legs, and the top of his head burning.

And then he heard a click and he opened his eyes, still breathing heavily.

The emergency lighting system had come on. Clearly, whatever Peter had done to the system, Smitts jamming the Taser on the cable had overridden that. Or maybe the backup would've always come on, eventually.

Fuck if he knew.

The room was awash in a grayish glow from the emergency lights above. A monitor also clicked on, just one, but it was something else that drew Ben's attention.

"Smitts!" he called out, before immediately scrambled toward his friend.

As he neared, his nose and mouth were accosted by the smell and taste of singed flesh.

"Oh god," he moaned. When he came within a foot of the body, he tried to reach out and grab Smitts, but he instinctively recoiled instead. "Oh god."

He turned back to his friend, but couldn't bring himself to hold the man.

Smitts's face was a molten mess, like an oversized beige candle having run its course. His eye sockets were filled with what looked like jelly, and his hair was a smoldering mess, revealing patches of red, almost glowing skin beneath.

Ben started to cry and gag at the same time.

He couldn't help either visceral reaction.

"Fuck, fuck, fuck—goddammit, Smitts."

Just under two days ago, the warden had been summoned from his office under the horrible circumstances of his friend being murdered.

Less than forty-eight hours later, every single one of his staff had been killed.

Every last one.

Still crying, Ben looked away from Smitts's face and turned back to Peter, who was slumped in a heap, his back pressed against the table, blood dripping down his chin.

"You fucking asshole," he sputtered, forcing himself to his feet. "You fucking crazy asshole."

Feeling the strain in both of his quads, the warden of Seaforth Prison gritted his teeth and made his way back to Peter's fallen body, scooping up the shotgun as he passed. He checked the chamber, too; the shotgun was of the pump-action variety, and it still had five shots left.

Ben walked right up to Peter; then, when he was hovering above him, he gritted his teeth and placed a heavy boot on the man's shoulder. Slowly, deliberately, he lowered the shotgun barrel until it was within inches of his smashed mouth.

Peter didn't move.

"I should blow your head off," he whispered. For a split second, his finger tensed on the trigger, and he turned his face to one side to avoid the brunt of the carnage that was about to ensue.

But then he put his finger on the guard.

He couldn't—no matter what Peter had done, he just couldn't kill the man in cold blood.

The hand not clutching the shotgun reached up and fondled the cross around his neck.

Father Callahan.

Every one of his guards died today, as well as most of his friends.

Except for one.

And he was here somewhere.

Ben wouldn't let the last man he cared about die in this prison.

Not today.

Not ever.

A flash of light in his periphery drew his gaze, and he lowered the shotgun while turning to face the monitor.

There, on screen, were four people he had never seen before standing in the entrance of Seaforth Prison.

And one of them was holding an automatic assault rifle.

The cavalry had arrived.

You're going to pay for this, Carson. You're going to fucking pay.

Chapter 30

THE LIGHTS CAME BACK on, but they were muted now; pervading the hallway in a dull gray glow. This didn't bother Father Callahan; after all, his eyes barely worked these days.

The aching priest shuffled along, noting the eerie silence of the prison. If he needed further affirmation, something in addition to the dreams and visions, seeing Quinn's quiddity roaming the halls, and the fact that it had been Carson Ford of all people that had killed him, then this was it: no prison should be this quiet, and definitely not one full of such hardened criminals as Seaforth.

In prisons, silence only happened in death and before a storm.

Father closed his eyes for a moment, and pushed away thoughts of his previous life that threatened to fill the silent void—thoughts about failed exorcisms, about time lost, about young boys that he couldn't protect. This was about the now, and now he needed to concentrate.

Eyes still closed, Callahan used his hands brushing against the walls as his guide. And he continued to keep his mind empty, blank, waiting for the power of the Marrow to envelop him. His breathing regulated, his eyelids, still closed, began to flutter, and the concrete wall against his calloused fingertips became a generalized sensation.

He's here—Carson's here, and…and there's someone else.

Father Callahan opened his eyes and was shocked to see a man standing before him. He was wearing a guard's uniform, the same navy blue that Ben Tristen had been sporting.

For once, the priest was grateful for his poor vision; the man's face was covered in bloody streaks, and there was something wrong with his eyes, but he couldn't make out the details.

"Are you...are you here to guide me?" Callahan asked uncertainly. It was ironic, of course, the blind leading the blind.

The man seemed confused by this, his face contorting.

"I think—" He cleared his throat. "I think I need to take you somewhere."

Father Callahan nodded and took a step forward, his old heart pumping harder now in his chest. Even as the keeper of the book, even knowing what he knew, Callahan still had to concentrate to see the quiddity; most of the time he knew they were there, but to actually *see* them required significant effort.

Most of the time he was content in just letting them pass by him without incident.

But not this time.

The dead guard slowly turned on his heels and began walking, his gait hitched, lacking the fluidity of normal movement. It was as if he were some sort of marionette.

And Father Callahan knew exactly who the puppeteer was in this puppet show of gore and pain.

The priest's hand slipped under his robe and he gripped the handle of the blade tucked beneath for comfort.

And to reassure himself that it was still there.

"Come," the guard said over his shoulder to the priest. "Please, come with me. They're waiting for you. They've been waiting a long, *long* time for you."

Father Callahan swallowed hard and took an uneasy step forward.

Without his guide, Father Callahan knew it unlikely that he would have been able to find his way to Cell Block E even if his

mind had been clear. Although not a particularly large prison—
what did Ben say? It holds twenty-two prisoners?—it was built in
such a way that made the course to Cell Block E unintuitive,
which was clearly intentional.

When they turned the final corner, Father Callahan felt a
pressure build inside his chest, and he knew that they were
close.

Sweat beaded on his forehead.

He was nervous. *So* nervous, and not for the first time he
began to question his motivations.

What if the book is wrong? What if all of this is wrong?

Callahan wiped the sweat from his brow with the back of his
hand. It was natural, he knew, during times of stress to question
one's faith. He wasn't the first to feel this way.

In fact, it wasn't even the first time for him.

A man of the cloth, the events that transpired all those years
had changed him. And when he had been given the book...that
had changed *everything*.

Back then, his challenge had been physical as well as mental.
Which was why he had put Robert up for adoption; he wasn't
fit to raise the boy, wasn't fit to even look after himself.

Especially not after what happened to Christine.

Images of the botched exorcism, of the poor junkie gagging,
spewing water, flooded his mind, and it was all he could do to
lift his leg and keep moving forward.

The guard suddenly stopped in front of him, and Callahan
snapped out of his head.

"Open the door," the man instructed.

Callahan squinted hard, unsure of who the man was speaking to.

"M—" *me?* he meant to ask, but then, after blinking rapidly
several times, he realized that he wasn't the intended target.

The scene before him suddenly came into focus. The guard wasn't speaking to one person, but *dozens*.

There were so many men, all dressed in identical white t-shirts and gray pants, that they seemed to almost make a wall.

A silent, unmoving wall of inmates.

Callahan shuddered with the realization.

This is why the prison is so quiet. All of the inmates are here, guarding Carson.

In the back of the priest's mind, he hoped that Ben was hiding somewhere, that he was okay.

Or that he'd managed to get out before all of *this*.

But despite the warnings he had issued the warden, he doubted it. Ben was as stubborn as he was devoted, and Callahan knew that he wouldn't leave this place. He was like a captain of his own personal ship—and whatever happened, he was destined to go down with it.

The men, heads still hung low, parted, allowing him passage to the door, which someone had opened. None of the men even acknowledged the priest.

A sudden calm came over Father Callahan, vanquishing any fear that he might have—*should* have—felt in their presence.

These men wouldn't hurt him, he knew; they wouldn't dare.

The inmates' faces were downcast, and they all looked the same to him. Sure, they were of different ethnicities, and they had different hairstyles, tattoos, scars, but in a way, they were all the same.

They were dangerous men, but they weren't the *most* dangerous in Seaforth.

Carson was—he ran the show here.

And for reasons that he couldn't fathom, Carson was allowing *him* passage.

Father Callahan's grip tightened on the handle of the hidden blade as he took a step forward.

The guard held the door open for him as Father passed through, and the priest waited for him to follow. But the man shook his head.

"No, I need to stay here," he said. "He has another job for me."

Father Callahan glanced down the long hallway before him, and nodded. There were maybe four or five wooden doors on the left-hand side, but despite never having been here, he was certain he knew which one Carson was housed in.

He could just feel it; he could feel it like a tug on his old bones, gentle teasing of the thin hair sitting atop his wrinkled scalp.

A pull on his quiddity deep inside him.

His *oneness.*

The priest turned back to face the blinded guard one final time just before the door closed.

Father Callahan swallowed hard, and then shuffled forward.

He didn't need his guide anymore. He was alone.

Alone to do one more job.

One more job to do. One. More. Job.

Chapter 31

"YOU KNOW WHERE TO go, Aiden—lead the way."

The man waved the light on the gun back and forth, working his way slowly down the narrow hallway, Sean following closely behind him. Robert hung back, shielding Shelly, who took up the rear.

Robert could hear as well as feel her breath on his neck, and it offered him strange comfort in the deathly quiet prison.

There was plenty that was not right at Seaforth—he didn't need any special dreams or powers of perception to tell him that.

Still, as he moved deeper into the silent prison, he *did* feel something…something in his chest, a tightness that at first he mistook for fatigue. But as they continued at a snail's pace led by Aiden and his assault rifle, the sensation grew stronger, and somewhere deep in his subconscious, he knew that it was the tug of the Marrow. The rift, or whatever Carson was doing, was messing with the air, rendering it thicker, making time move more slowly. He had felt this several times before, Robert realized—in the basement of the Harlop Estate with James, and in the cabin in the woods with George—but back then he had passed it off as…well, as something he didn't quite understand. But now, imbued with new knowledge that Sean had shared with him, he knew what it was.

Every spirit that stayed in this world brought a little bit of the Marrow with them.

And here, in *this* place, there were a lot of spirits.

And this wasn't a good thing.

Shelly's breathing suddenly became more rapid, and he chanced a look over his shoulder at her. Her pretty red lips were pressed together tightly and her eyes had a strange vacant look to them.

"You feel that, too?" he whispered.

Her eyes cleared.

"No," she answered quickly, and Robert instantly knew that she was lying. The question was: why? Why would she lie about it? But before he could challenge her, Aiden's voice drew him back.

"Hold," he instructed, holding up a closed fist. They were at a bifurcation in the hallway, the left leading to what looked like an exterior door, the yard, perhaps, while the right had a sign above reading Mess Hall. It dawned on Robert that here, in this place, they weren't only going to have to be on watch for quiddity, but for mass murderers as well. He hoped that the latter were tucked away in their cells, sleeping for the night, but from what he had seen in movies, prisons were *never* this quiet.

One could hope, but one could just as easily deceive themselves. In Robert's experience, they were one and the same, and both were recipes for disaster.

"What is it?" he whispered, but Sean hushed him.

Aiden kept his gun light trained on the door to the mess hall. For nearly a full minute, the four of them just stood in the hallway and waited. And then, just as Robert's nerve was about to fray, the door slowly opened.

Robert felt his blood run cold.

A man, his face buried in his hands, his posture stooped, walked through the door as if on a Sunday afternoon stroll.

As if all was right in the world.

"What the—?"

But Sean hushed him again. The man in the uniform didn't seem to notice them as he continued toward them.

Robert's heart was racing now, and he waited with clenched teeth, trying to guess what was going to happen next. If he should act, do *something*.

Is this a prisoner who stole guard's clothing? Is Aiden going to open fire?

He could feel Shelly press up against him from behind, and together their heartbeats set their bodies rocking.

This is so fucked, this is so fucked, this is so fucked...why isn't he doing anything?

And then the man started to laugh, and Robert nearly lost it. It was a horrible, monotone sound that grated on his very soul.

"Stop," Aiden instructed, waving his gun back and forth.

The emergency lights suddenly clicked and the man turned his face skyward. It was only then that Robert noticed the man's hands were covered in blood. And when he pulled his hands away from his face, he realized that this was no inmate, but the guard that had been murdered.

A gasp escaped him.

The man's eye sockets were hollow, empty. Shelly's arms clenched his waist so tightly that he had a hard time taking a deep breath.

"Stop!" Aiden instructed again. Unlike Robert and Shelly, he seemed unfazed by the man's horrific appearance.

Just as the man seemed unfazed by Aiden and his gun; he kept walking toward them.

A sound to their right, a heavy exhalation, suddenly drew Robert's gaze.

"Sean!" he shouted, but his warning was too late.

Inset on the hard, concrete wall was a small door that they had passed only seconds ago, which, at the time, had been firmly closed. Now, however, it was flung and a man lunged from the interior, his body like a spear aimed directly at Sean's side.

Sean swiveled, as did Aiden, but both men were too slow. The man, who had a shaved head covered in blue tattoos, struck Sean in the side, sending him flying across the hallway. He grunted when his back smashed into the wall, and the pistol fell from his hand and clattered to the ground. Robert shoved Shelly backward and together they spun away from the crazed inmate.

"Sean!" someone shouted.

Sean somehow managed to extricate himself from the man's grip, and then, breathing heavily and with his right arm hanging uselessly at his side, he tried to circle away.

But the man with the tattoos was like a caged animal, his eyes glinting even in the terrible lighting, a snarl etched on his hard face. He leapt at Sean once more, and despite receiving a solid uppercut to the jaw, the blond man was once again driven to the ground.

"Aiden!" Sean yelled. But Aiden was already on them, moving Robert and Shelly even farther away from the brawl.

Aiden didn't hesitate. He drove the toe of his boot into the man's ribs, sending an audible crack up and down the hallway. The man rocked to one side, which offered just enough separation between the two men for Aiden to safely fire.

The hallway erupted in a thunderstorm. The sound of the gunfire—a resonating *trrtt-trrtt-trrtt*—rattled Robert's molars, while the bright flash from the muzzle sent fireflies scattering across his vision.

The man's bald head was no longer blue with tattoos. In fact, Robert couldn't see his head at all; it had exploded into a spray of red and white and gray, soaking Sean, who was still partially beneath him.

"Oh god," Shelly moaned.

Robert felt like he was going to be sick, and turned away from the inmate's corpse.

Despite the ringing in his ears, he slowly began to pick up another sound.

The sound of laughter.

The guard!

Robert whipped around just in time to see the eyeless guard reaching out for Shelly, his fingers mere inches from her shoulder. Unlike Robert, she was transfixed on the dead man on the ground, watching in horror as blood continued to pump and spurt from his ragged stump of a neck.

They had forgotten all about the man with no eyes.

"No!" Robert screamed as he tried to pull Shelly away. But the guard continued to reach for her.

Robert felt the tightness in his chest grow to a level that was nearly unbearable, as if the blow that Sean had delivered to the inmate's jaw had connected with his solar plexus.

"Stop!" he shouted as loudly as he could, holding up one hand.

And then something strange happened.

The laughter stopped, the man's blood-streaked face went slack, and he instantly became still.

Chapter 32

"GET UP," BEN ORDERED. "Get the fuck up."

Peter spat a mixture of teeth and blood onto the floor.

Most of it ended up on the front of his guard uniform.

"Up. Now."

To emphasize his point, he delivered a soft kick to the man's leg. This spurred him to action, and Peter got to his feet, which was awkward given that Ben had bound his hands behind his back with some zip ties he had found in the desk.

"You don't know what you're doing," Peter said, his words slurred from his smashed mouth. "This is bigger than you."

Ben shoved him forward, then stepped behind him.

"Shut the fuck up," he ordered. For good measure, he pushed the end of the shotgun into the man's spine. Then he adjusted the other shotgun across his chest and made sure that the Taser and pistol were still on his hip. "Now move."

Peter took two steps forward, then slid to his right to avoid Smitts's burnt body. Ben himself averted his eyes, trying desperately to remain focused and avoid feeling more of the nagging guilt.

Before binding Peter, he had forced the man to switch the images on the monitors. Eventually they'd found Father Callahan.

The priest was at the door to Cell Block E, and Ben watched in awe as first the inmates parted, then the door seemed to open on its own.

And that was where Ben was headed now.

He had to save his friend.

Switching the monitors again, Peter had located the other men—including the one that was clearly military, followed by what looked like admin and two civilians—as they made their way into the main hallway, but then he had lost them.

"Move, Peter. You're leading the way."

Seaforth's head of IT took several more steps forward, but then he stopped abruptly.

"They'll kill me, you know. They'll kill you, too. They don't care—"

Somewhere far below them, a sound erupted, a deep, resonating buzzing. Only it wasn't a buzz-saw.

Ben knew that sound, and he knew it well.

It was the man in black's automatic rifle.

The warden's expression suddenly hardened.

"Move, Peter. Move *now!*"

Chapter 33

ROBERT WASN'T SURE WHAT had happened. One minute he was certain that the quiddity was going to grab Shelly and take her to the Marrow, and the next he seemed locked in place, unable to move.

"Robert?" Shelly asked quietly. She sidled up beside him, slowly, carefully, weary that any sudden movement might break whatever spell had fallen over the dead guard. "What's going on? What did you do to him?"

Robert didn't answer, partly because the pain in his chest had grown to immense proportions, and partly because he had no fucking clue what was going on.

"Who are you?" Robert asked. In his periphery, he picked up Sean and Aiden flanking him, guns raised. Even Sean, who must have known that his pistol would do no good against the dead, aimed the barrel directly at the guard's head.

"My...my name's Quinn," the man said.

"You were a guard here?" Sean asked over Robert's shoulder.

The man nodded.

"Worked here for seventeen years. Worked here until...until...a few days ago?"

The end of the man's sentence made it sound more like a question than a statement.

"And what happened a few days ago?" Sean pressed. Robert, his chest still tight to the point of making it difficult to breath, wondered where this line of question was going...and what the point was.

Whatever his intention, Robert hoped that Sean got to it quickly, because he had a feeling that as soon as the pain in his chest became too great and he lowered his hand, Quinn would be on the move again. And then there was no telling what would happen.

"I—I—I don't know," he stammered.

"Why did you come at us? Why were you laughing?"

"I don't—"

Something in the man's face suddenly changed, as if he suddenly remembered.

"The man in black," he whispered, and Robert felt his chest tighten again.

Leland Black.

"He told me to...told me that—"

"That's enough," Sean instructed.

"He told me that if I didn't, that if I let you guys interfere, then he would bring the girl."

"Enough!"

"Wait, what girl?" Robert interjected.

"Robert, we have to go."

Quinn shook his head violently from side to side.

"He said that if I brought the priest—"

"The priest?" This time it was Shelly who interrupted.

Robert's chest suddenly crunched, and he let out a grunt. He couldn't hold this man for much longer.

"Leland said he needed the priest to open the gate. The rift— I don't really know—"

Robert shook his head and asked his question through gritted teeth.

"What girl?"

"Robert—"

"What fucking girl?" he demanded with the last of his strength.

An odd silence fell over them.

Eventually, the man answered, and Robert, oddly confident that he would no longer attack them, lowered his hand.

Whatever hold Leland had had on this man, Robert had broken in.

"Amy. He said a girl named Amy would come, and that she would bring the demons with her."

Robert bent over at the waist, and then he stood up straight, sucking in a giant breath of air. His throat and lungs burned as if he was breathing in caustic fumes.

"Amy," he gasped. He felt Shelly grab hold of his shoulders, but he shrugged her off.

Quinn, now able to move, took a step backward.

"Sean," he gasped, "what the hell is he talking about?"

"We need to go, Robert—we need to stop Father Callahan."

Sean tried to push past him, but Robert held out his arm. The man, still fearful of his touch, stopped just short of making contact.

"Tell me what he's talking about. How does he know about Amy?"

Sean sighed and lowered his gun.

"There is more to the prophecy in the book, in *Inter vivos et mortuos.*"

Robert's eyes narrowed and he took another breath, the pressure in his chest easing a little more.

"Sean—you better tell me what the fuck this man is talking about," Robert threatened.

Sean's eyes bored into him. Robert stood his ground, and the man eventually looked away.

"The prophecy isn't just about Leland, Robert. It also speaks of a young girl, born of Guardians of great power, who holds the rift in the Marrow open. *She* is the one that brings the evil back to earth."

Robert could do nothing but gape at Sean. His face and upper body were completely covered in blood and gore from the inmate that had been blown away, but he barely noticed.

"*What?*"

Sean said nothing. For a second time, Shelly tried to grab Robert, but again he shook her off.

"I told you all I know."

Robert gritted his teeth, and felt his anger start to bubble over.

"You motherfucker! You never told me any of this! Amy! *Amy?*"

Sean's eyes flicked up.

"I wasn't supposed to tell you anything," the man yelled back.

Robert wasn't one for violence, but he was on the precipice of striking the man.

"You weren't *supposed* to? What the fuck is that supposed to mean?"

He moved right into Sean's face.

"What the fuck—?"

Shelly grabbed his arm, and this time he thrust her away angrily. She stumbled backward and bumped hard against the back wall.

Robert ignored her—he was too far gone now.

"It was in the book," Sean said simply.

"This fucking book! Give *me* the fucking book!"

"I don't have it."

Aiden, who had been standing silently the whole time, his gun trained on the door to the mess hall, spat a wad of dip to the floor.

"Someone's moving," he said.

Nobody took notice.

"Who has this goddamn book, then?"

"Father Callahan."

Robert's eyes narrowed.

"The fucking priest? The priest who's here somewhere?"

Sean nodded.

"Then we'll just have to go get it."

Sean opened his mouth to say something, but then closed it.

"What? Say it, Sean. Just fucking say it."

"Robert, your daughter—"

Robert saw red and lashed out with his fist. His knuckles connected with the side of Sean's face with a resounding crack. Pain shot up his hand and he immediately shook his fist at his side.

Sean stumbled backward, then righted himself.

He didn't rub his jaw.

"Don't you ever speak of her again, do you hear me? Sean, do you—?"

But another voice, a familiar male voice, suddenly spoke from behind him, and he froze.

"Robert? You're glowing, Robert. You're *glowing*."

Robert spun on his heels and then almost fell to the ground.

He couldn't believe his eyes.

There was a kid standing behind Shelly, whose eyes, nearly hidden behind circular spectacles, were moist, and he was holding a camera in his hands.

Beside the kid was Robert's best friend in the world.

And Cal looked worse than he had ever seen him.

Chapter 34

THE HALLWAY WAS DARK and damp and reeked of brine. Father Callahan's pace slowed as he neared the final door to the room, realizing that he was on the verge of meeting the man — just a boy then — that he had abandoned more than two decades prior.

And he was going to kill him, because he had to.

He was nervous, not for his own life, but of failing.

Father Callahan put a hand on the door to the cell and took a deep breath. Then he closed his eyes. Even though he had since moved on from his God, he fell into old habits and started to pray, even though there were no gods of the Marrow to hear him.

Our Father, who art —

"Come in, Callahan, the door is unlocked."

The priest's cataractous eyes snapped open.

It was time. And he was ready.

Father Callahan pushed the hard wooden door, and it slowly started to open. Then he stepped inside.

The room was as he had seen on the monitor with Ben what seemed like a decade ago now: small, square, nondescript. Although in the video there had been a bed and toilet in the room, those were gone now, likely removed by the inmates that were guarding Cell Block E.

Even the man's clothes, previously balled in the corner of the room, were gone.

Carson Ford was sitting with his back to Father Callahan, his legs crossed in front of him, his hands resting gently on his thighs. The man was unassuming in stature, his thin body accentuated by the vertebrae that jutted from his skin. He was covered in bruises, which Callahan assumed were from the guards—minor vengeance after what had happened to their friend and colleague.

There was also a strange hum in the air, and a tightness in his chest that he had felt in the hallway began to intensify.

"Carson," he said softly, but his words incited no reaction from the man. Father Callahan resisted the urge to reach through his robe and grab the knife therein.

It would be easy to pull it out, then trace a line across the man's throat as he sat with his back to him.

Too easy.

Which meant that Carson had something up his sleeve. A card to play.

A wild card.

The devil will confuse, confound with his tricks.

"Carson," he said again, hoping that this time the man would turn.

He did not.

The man's back expanded as he took a particularly deep breath, then his whole body shook as if he were an athlete trying to get loose before an event.

"Father Callahan, I've been waiting for you."

This time, Father Callahan couldn't resist the urge to slip his hand inside his robe and grab the handle of the knife.

"But before we get started, I have a few questions for you. Would that be okay?"

Carson's politeness threw Father Callahan off guard. The man before him didn't seem like a psychopathic murderer.

The devil's tricks.

"Father?"

"Yes?"

"May I ask you a few questions?"

Father Callahan's grip tightened and he took a few steps forward. He was only four feet from the man's back now, so close that he could smell the reek of the man's sweat.

"Yes," he replied softly.

"Thank you, Father."

Carson cleared his throat.

"Do you remember that day? That day in the summer when we first met?"

Despite trying to ignore the man's words, to remain focused, an image of Sean Sommers at his church door all those years ago flashed in his mind nonetheless.

"Yes, yes, I remember," he admitted.

"Do you think that if you had taken me instead of Robert, things would be different?"

Another image, this time of the two boys, one in each of Sean's hands. Twin boys.

Father Callahan didn't answer the question, because he didn't know.

How could he?

Carson laughed.

"What about both of us, then? What if you had taken both of us, found a nice home for me as well as my brother? Did you ever think of that?"

Callahan swallowed hard. Ever since he had first heard of Carson Ford, and realized who he really was, these very thoughts had coursed through his head. And the guilt had eaten him up for years.

It still ate at his quiddity to this day.

He *could* have taken both—if only he had known then who they were. If he had just known more, if Sean had just told him more, had helped him translate the book, he *would* have taken both.

Instead, he had only taken Robert. And he had failed even this boy, shipping him off with foster parents so that Leland couldn't find him again.

And then *he* had found Leland; he and the other Guardians.

Father Callahan refused to think of what happened next.

"Oh, please, Father, don't feel compelled to answer. Consider these," he laughed again, "simple musings of a madman. After all, most everyone else has. Even your friend Ben, he thinks I'm mad. Refuses to listen."

Father Callahan was in the process of taking another step forward, but hesitated at the mention of his friend's name.

"But you, Father. You are different. You *know* things, you've seen them. You've felt them. You probably feel them now...a tightness in your chest, perhaps? Or slowing of time?"

Callahan tried not to pay attention to what the man was saying, but he found himself unable to resist.

Carson laughed again.

"That's okay, Father. Like I said, you don't have to answer. But I want to tell you a story...would that be okay?"

"Yes," Callahan croaked. His throat suddenly felt incredibly dry, no matter how many times he swallowed.

From behind, he could see Carson nod ever so slightly.

"You know, at first, I killed for vengeance, revenge. That's it—there wasn't any deeper meaning to it. I stabbed my stepfather in the chest after he had put a cigar out on my arm. Then I slit my stepmother's throat."

Carson shrugged.

"That's when I learned I liked it. I suppose deep down it was a control thing—not being able to control anything in my life, I exerted my control over others instead, in the most fundamental of ways. By taking their lives. Me 'n' Buddy used to do that—shit, we did that *a lot*. But it wasn't until my eighth or ninth kill that I actually watched them die. *Really* watched them. And that was when I saw something in their faces, something that I knew shouldn't have been there. A release of sorts."

Callahan inched forward.

"And this got me to thinking…thinking about realization, about self-awareness. I spent considerable time contemplating the fact that humans *know* we are alive, that we *know* we are conscious, self-aware. This really is a fucked-up thing, if you put some thought into it. Don't you agree, Father?"

Callahan paused, hoping that the question was rhetorical.

It wasn't.

"Father? It *is* fucked up, wouldn't you agree?"

"It is…unique."

Carson laughed.

"Certainly one way of putting it. We are the only beings that are self-aware, that much is certain. But it's also *fucked*. I mean, when I was growing up, trying to live off dumpster scraps, trying to stay away from the junkie that prick Sean left me with and her abusive pimp, I *knew* that I was fucked. That I hurt. That I—" For the first time since Father Callahan had entered the room, Carson moved one of his hands. He brought his right index finger to his chest. "—I hurt. I knew I was getting the short end of the stick, you know? But the question I always had, even though I couldn't articulate it back then, was *why* I knew this. And that's when I started to learn about the Marrow. That was when my real father, when Leland, started speaking to me."

At the mention of the Goat's name, Father Callahan took a deep breath.

"Exactly. Scary bastard, isn't he? But he also told me about you, Father. Which is why I knew that eventually you would come. When the barrier between the Marrow and this world started to weaken, I knew that you would come."

Then Carson laughed, and Father Callahan knew that he could wait no longer. He slipped the knife out of from beneath his robes and strode forward as quickly as his ancient body would allow. In as fluid a movement as he could muster, he reached forward, placed his hand on Carson's forehead, and pulled back, while at the same time pressing the tip of the blade against the man's bare throat.

It was Carson's lack of reaction that caused Father Callahan to hesitate. He should have just buried the blade deep in his neck and got it over with.

But Carson just smiled, as if he knew this was coming all along.

And perhaps he *had* known.

"Do it," the man hissed. "Kill me, Father. I have no fear of death—I know which choice I will make on the shores of the Marrow. The question is, do you, Father? Father Callahan, are you ready to eradicate yourself? Or will you join us in the flames?"

Chapter 35

BEN TRIPLE CHECKED THE shotguns and pistol before leaving the room. His system was flooded with adrenaline, in a way that was foreign to him. Sure, as warden of Seaforth Prison, he was always on edge, prepared for anything from the inmates, but this was different. Ben was typically on the defense, ready to react rather than act.

But today was different.

Today he was on the offensive.

"Step aside," he instructed Peter. The man did as he was instructed, head bowed. Ben stepped forward and swiped his keycard on the door.

It worked, which came as a welcome surprise. Evidently when Smitts had fried the circuit board with the Taser and the emergency power had come back on, it had reset whatever fucked-up virus Peter had infected the system with.

He pulled the door wide, and then held it open with his foot. "Move."

Peter stepped in front of him, traipsing through the blood on the stairs where Smitts had been stabbed.

Fucking Smitts…fucking Quinn…fucking Callahan.

Ben fought the tears away again.

As a veteran of two wars, Ben Tristen was no stranger to seeing friends and comrades fall. But today was different. Back then he had been a fucking grunt, obeying orders as they all did, no matter how inane. But today, *here* at Seaforth, he was in charge. And those who died today did so on his watch—under his command.

"Fuck," he murmured.

Blinking rapidly to clear his vision, he pushed the muzzle of the shotgun into Peter's back again, forcing him forward.

When they reached the bottom of the stairs, he half expected Carson to peek his head around as he had when Smitts had been stabbed, and his finger tensed on the trigger of the shotgun.

But there was no one there.

He half believed that he had made that up, just like he had made up that he had seen Quinn after he had died. But the other half of him...

*Smitts said he saw him...*Smitts, *of all people.*

And then there was what Peter and Father Callahan had said. All that bullshit about Carson and some fucked-up afterlife.

Ben shook his head and opened the door at the bottom of the stairwell. To be safe, he shoved Peter through first, crouching behind him, the shotgun armed and ready.

Nothing.

No more gunfire, which had drawn him from the control room in the first place.

Still, as they made their way down the hallway toward Cell Block E, Warden Ben Tristen kept the shotgun at the ready.

After all, there were more than two dozen mass murderers in Seaforth.

And only one priest, armed with only his wit and a strange, burning desire to speak to the worst of them all.

Chapter 36

"CAL? WHAT IN THE living *fuck* are you doing here?"

Robert blinked twice, convinced that what he was seeing was a strange mirage. His hand still throbbed from where he had punched Sean, and for a moment he thought that perhaps the man had hit him back...and knocked him out cold, making this all a fucked-up dream. But then Cal answered, and he knew that his friend was here, in the flesh.

"I...Sean brought me here with Allan."

Robert couldn't believe his ears.

"What?"

Sean stepped forward and Robert was tempted to punch him again.

How the fuck could he bring Cal here? And Allan? The fucking kid with the camera?

And then he remembered what Sean had said as they had arrived at the outer gates of Seaforth.

Strange, the keycard worked before...

"A long time ago, I told you that you were *selected*. But I would be a fool to put all my eggs in one basket. Don't you see, Robert? Why the fuck can't you see?" Sean waved his arms about the hallway. "This is bigger than you, bigger than me, bigger than all of us."

Robert glared at the man.

"Yeah, but Cal? Where the fuck have you been? What the *fuck* were you thinking?"

"What is that supposed to mean?"

Robert whipped around, directing his icy stare at his friend.

"What I mean is that you shouldn't be here, Cal. And you shouldn't have brought the kid."

Allan moved a spectacled eye from behind the camera lens, which Robert noticed was still aimed directly at him.

You're glowing, Robert.

"I'm eighteen," Allan informed them, but the comment went ignored.

"Robbo, Sean asked me to help. What was I supposed to do? Besides" — he hooked a chin at Shelly — "you two were too busy fucking to care about any of this."

"What?"

Robert took a step forward, his fists clenching. Cal didn't back down.

"There's someone coming," Aiden repeated, but like Allan, no one paid attention to him either.

Cal stuck his gut out.

"You heard me."

"You think this is a fucking game, Cal? Is that it? You pissed because Shelly picked me instead of you? So this is — what — some sort of payback?"

Cal threw his arms up.

"Not everything is about you, you narcissistic prick. This is about the fucking Marrow, Robbo. Can't you see that? You're standing here, getting pissed off at Sean, at this fucking dead guy here, pushing Shelly against the wall. You think it's all about you. Sorry, bro. It ain't."

Robert chewed the inside of his cheek so hard that he tasted blood.

"It *is* about me," he spat. "It's about me, because *my* daughter. It's about me because — " He hiked up his jean leg, revealing the three talon-shaped scars. " — because Leland touched me. And last, but not fucking least, it's about me because Leland is my father. That, my good friend *Cal*, is why it's about me right now."

Cal was floored, and a silence fell over the room. Robert was breathing heavily, trying to regain control. Everything had happened so quickly, from the information that Sean had given him in the helicopter, to the dead guard talking about Amy, that he felt himself spiraling out of control.

A loud bang suddenly erupted from somewhere behind him, and he whipped around in time to see the door to the mess hall swing wide, and a shadowy figure running toward them.

Allan swung the camera from Robert to the figure, and the viewfinder remained dark.

"He's alive!" Allan shouted.

Which was true, but only for another moment.

Aiden stepped up, bent on one knee, and opened fire.

The man's chest erupted in a spray of blood, his momentum sending his limbs forward while his core was thrust backward.

Someone screamed—for all Robert knew, it was him.

The gore was too much, and he retched.

Everything was too much.

"More on their way," Aiden said matter-of-factly. He spat some tobacco juice onto the floor. "We have to move."

But Robert's feet felt like they were rooted in cement. He couldn't move. Someone's arm rested on his back, but he was too tired, too confused, to shake it off this time. He just hoped it was Shelly and not Cal.

"Move," Aiden repeated.

And then Robert felt it. The pressure in his chest again, like he had felt when he had ordered the dead guard to stay. He also felt time slowing.

Something was definitely happening here at Seaforth. And if his difficulty breathing was any indication, it was happening soon.

"We need to hurry," he managed to croak, straightening himself. "We need to find Carson fast."

Sean nodded, then turned to the dead guard.

"You know where he is?"

The man nodded.

"Still in his cell."

"Good; take us there. Aiden, you first." He turned to Allan next. "That camera pick up quiddity? Is that what you said?"

Allan nodded, his eyes huge and bulging behind his glasses. There was vomit on his chin and more of it clinging to his t-shirt.

"Yes, when there are quiddity onscreen, they glow a—"

"You follow Aiden, let us know if the bogies are human or dead." He turned to Robert next. "And you, if they're dead, do whatever the fuck you just did to Quinn. The rest of you, get behind us. Stay close, stay tight. I'll take up the rear."

Aiden spat again.

"Fire at will?"

Sean nodded, pulling out his pistol.

"Fire at will," he confirmed.

They quickly regrouped, and then Aiden crossed the threshold into the mess hall.

Chapter 37

FATHER CALLAHAN'S HANDS WERE shaking, and the sweat on his palms was threatening to cause the blade to slip out from his grip.

The pressure in his chest was immense, almost bone-crushing.

Carson laughed.

"Nervous? Why are you nervous? *She* isn't even here yet."

She?

At first, he thought Carson was referring to the girl in the prophecy, the one that would hold the rift open for the demons to spew forth. But the next sentence from the killer's mouth banished the idea.

"Christine, why don't you step forward?"

Father Callahan's hand slipped off Carson's forehead, and the man lowered his gaze.

"No...no...it can't be..."

As the shape of the woman began to materialize in the corner of the otherwise empty room, Father Callahan let go of Carson and stumbled backward.

The woman was thin, with wiry black hair. Her flesh was pale, her eyes milky, and there were red sores on the insides of her arms: track marks.

"It can't be," he stammered again.

"Oh, it can be, Father—it *is*."

The woman took a step forward, then another. Father Callahan, eyes bulging, matched her step for step until his back bumped up against the wooden door to the cell. And when it did, the blade fell from his hand and clattered to the floor. Any altruistic ideas of sacrificing himself, of doing anything and everything it took to prevent Carson from opening the rift, melted away.

"Say hi, Christine," Carson instructed as he rose to his feet and finally turned to face the priest.

Christine opened her decaying mouth to say something, but the only thing that came out was a heavy burping sound. As Father Callahan watched and listened in sheer horror, the sound transitioned into something moist and bubbly. And then water spewed forth from her mouth, soaking the front of her filthy t-shirt.

"No!" Father Callahan screamed.

"Oh, yes. See, even people like you have demons, stuff in their past that they regret, don't they? You remember Christine, don't you? I mean, you thought she was possessed, am I right?" Carson laughed and Christine, mouth still spewing a geyser of foul-smelling water, continued to shamble forward.

Father Callahan turned around and fumbled with the door, trying desperately to open it.

"Yeah, you remember her. Of course you do. Tried to exorcise her demon...by, what? Waterboarding her? Wasn't that it?" He laughed. "You sadistic bastard. She wasn't possessed...she was addicted to drugs, Callahan. But I guess you know that now. Don't you?"

Despite his efforts, the priest couldn't manage to open the door. Desperate, he scratched at the wood around the lock, causing splinters to embed beneath his nails. His heart was beating so hard in his chest that he felt like his whole body was thrumming like a plucked violin string.

"It's locked, Father," Carson said, suddenly sounding bored.

When his fingers were reduced to a bloody, raw mess, Father Callahan gave up and turned around. Christine was within three feet of him now. Unable to deal with the sight of her, he slid to the hard floor. Out of the corner of his eye, he caught sight of the blade, which was just within reach. As Christine stepped forward, water still pouring from her mouth, Callahan stretched and grabbed the blade. The horrible fluid splashed down on his head, soaking him.

He gagged; the water, if that was what it was, was foul and thicker than he first thought. Father Callahan turned his eyes upward, but had to quickly look away as the water cascaded down over his face.

"*Tsk, tsk,* Father. You should know better — that blade won't do anything to Christine...she's already dead."

Father Callahan retched, and then moved his head to one side, out of the direct flow of infinite water from Christine's maw.

"It's not for her," he wheezed. And then he brought the blade up to his own neck. "It's for me!"

The smile suddenly fell off Carson's face.

"No!" he screamed at the top of his lungs. "Christine! Stop him!"

Chapter 38

"THIS WAY, QUICKLY!" THE guard said, waving them through the open doorway.

Aiden went first, followed by Sean, then Robert, then the others.

It was the third doorway that they had been through in the last several minutes, and Robert was beginning to think that they were going in circles.

"How much farther?" he asked quietly.

The guard shook his head.

"Not far, but like I said, we have to go through the mess hall and then deal with the inmates. They are guarding Carson. I don't know what he promised them, but they are...they are..."

Aiden suddenly held up his fist as they came up to another door.

"Mess hall," the guard confirmed.

Aiden nodded.

"Uhh, guys?" a small voice asked.

Aiden looked over at Sean, and glanced down at his gun. Sean raised the pistol and nodded back.

"Guys?"

"I'll take right, you left. Shoot on sight."

"Guys!"

Robert finally turned and found himself staring into Allan's pale face.

"What?"

"You should—you should see this."

Robert didn't move. Cal did the honors and flipped the viewfinder of the kid's camera around, the aperture of which was still pointed directly at the door.

Robert's heart immediately sunk.

"Jesus," he whispered. "Can it be a mistake?"

Allan shook his head slowly.

"How many?" Sean asked in his usual monotone voice.

"I—I—"

"Allan! How many are there?"

"I don't know! Too many, can't even see the separation."

The viewfinder was awash in red and yellow light. It was as if the entire mess hall was glowing.

Aiden looked to Sean for advice, then to Robert.

"Plan?" he said simply.

Sean turned to Robert.

"Can you do that thing again? Make them stop? Stand still?"

Robert shrugged.

"Fuck if I know. I don't even know what I did."

Sean stared at him for a good five seconds before turning to the guard.

"Any other way to Cell Block E? To Carson?"

The man shook his head, who Robert still couldn't stare at directly given the fact that his eyes had been torn from his head.

"Through the mess hall is the only way."

Sean chewed his lip, uncertain for one of only a few times since Robert had met the man. But whatever he decided, Robert hoped that he would hurry. The pressure in his chest was building again, and time had once again acquired the strange, liquid-like quality that Robert was becoming all too familiar with.

"We have to move," he instructed the group. "I'll go first."

Shelly grabbed the back of his arm, and when he turned to face her, he realized that there were tears in her eyes.

"Rob, you can't."

Robert looked to Cal next, who couldn't quite meet his gaze. He felt horrible for the way he had treated his friends—his only friends in this world.

He nodded, standing up tall.

"I can, and I will. Like you said"—he looked at Cal—"it isn't all about me."

The guard spoke next.

"I'll go with," he said.

Robert turned back to the door before either Cal or Shelly could protest.

Sean was staring at him, and judging by the pained expression on his face, the man was also feeling the pressure in his chest.

"You two go in, then me and Aiden, in case there are inmates in there, too." The man turned to the other members of their crew and stared at them for a moment. Even though he said nothing, Robert knew what he was thinking. Sean was debating whether or not to order them to stay here—if that would be safer. "You guys stay close," the man decided at last.

Then he whipped around to face the door, moving off to one side to allow Robert to pass.

Robert took another deep breath with his eyes closed. He could feel the pressure building, and knew inside that he could do what he had done to the guard again, no matter how many ghosts there were inside.

After all, he wasn't just a Guardian, but he was Leland's son.

And Amy's father.

Robert exhaled and shoved the door to the mess hall wide.

Chapter 39

REALIZING HE HAD BEEN duped, that Carson and Leland had lured him here, that they needed him to open the gate, there was only one decision that he could make. There was only one way to stop them.

But Father Callahan was old and slow.

Too slow.

Christine reached down and grabbed his arm a split second before he plunged the blade into his neck. And then everything started to go black.

The priest felt his body tense, as if every muscle in his body had seized all at once. And then, as the fluid finally stopped pouring out of Christine's mouth, he found himself staring into her eyes, unable to move, unable to breathe.

Her eyes started to go dark, the whites disappearing into a solid black. But as he watched, he realized that there were flecks of white in those eyes, flecks that soon started to grow and grow, until they weren't just flecks, but a froth of some sort.

The Marrow, he thought. The word brought with it a calmness that started to flow over and through him all at once.

But then he heard a voice.

"Oh no you don't. Not yet, Father."

Someone gripped his other arm, and the feeling that was previously contained inside him now poured out and into Carson.

The naked murderer moaned, and his whole body shuddered.

"Yes, yes...the rift shall be opened," he called out, his voice bordering on ecstasy.

Father Callahan opened his eyes, and realized that he had been moved to the center of the room, and now he was lying on his back, his arms spread out at his sides.

Christine was on his right, while Carson was on his left, both seated, both holding one of his hands in their laps.

Carson had a sinister grin on his face, and in that instant Father Callahan knew that he had failed. Worse, he had given Carson what he needed to open the rift; he was the keeper of the book, and now, holding Carson's living hand, and Christine's dead hand, he was trapped between worlds.

And because of this, he would act as a conduit for the dead.

He was the rift.

How could I be so foolish? How could I be so stupid?

Father Callahan closed his eyes.

You did the right thing, Father. This is for the best.

His eyes snapped open.

The thought was in his head, but it wasn't his own. But it was one that he recognized.

It was from a man that he and Sean had chased for nearly a decade, a man that they had stolen two sons from.

Thank you, Father Callahan. Thank you.

"I—" Father Callahan croaked, but his head was suddenly thrown back, and his mouth was thrust open. "Noooooo!"

Light shot from his eyes and open mouth, turning his entire world white.

"Yes, yes, it's opening," he heard someone say, although he couldn't tell if the words were in his head, or if it was Carson or Christine speaking. "It's *opening!*"

The pressure in the priest's chest suddenly eased, and he felt a moment of odd relaxation. It was as if his body had melted and he was finally unburdened of his aches and pains. His robes tore, and out of his bare chest came a massive beam of light that shot to the ceiling, where it puddled and frothed on the cement like the flames in the Marrow that he had read about but had never seen for himself.

And then his ribcage separated and pulled apart. He tried to scream, but only more light, *brighter* light, came out of his mouth.

The floor beneath his body fell away, revealing a roiling sea crashing on caramel shores.

And fire, there was fire there, too.

There was fire everywhere.

Thank you, Father, thank you, thank you, thank you...

Chapter 40

IT WAS A GRUESOME scene that Robert wasn't prepared for, despite the horrors that he had already witnessed on this day.

There were nearly a dozen men hanging from the rafters, crude nooses made of various materials from bedsheets to what looked like electrical cords wrapped around their necks. Their mouths were agape, tongues lolling, eyes bulging. The mess hall reeked something fierce, the bowels of the hanged having since let go.

"Oh my god," the guard whispered. "All of them...all of the guards are dead...my friends...my..."

Robert couldn't understand how this had happened.

How is it possible that every single guard in Seaforth Prison has been murdered?

"My god," the guard whispered again.

Robert felt his stomach lurch, but then the tightness in his chest came again, pushing the former sensation away.

Trying not to look at any of the faces of the dead, Robert strode into the mess hall, his palms up in front and slightly to the sides, ready to do...to do whatever the hell he had done to the guard, had done to Quinn.

There was a gasp from behind him, followed by the sound of someone retching violently.

"Camera up! Get the fucking camera up!" Sean shouted.

Robert took another step forward, weaving out of the way of one of the hanging corpses. Eyes peeled, he continued to walk, slowly, tentatively, his eyes locked on the door at the far end of the room.

The tightness in his chest grew, and now he heard something as well. The familiar sound of rushing waves could be heard underlying their heavy breathing.

Robert didn't know how, but Carson had done it; he had opened the rift.

"We need to hurry," Robert shouted. "We need—"

"Quiddity!" Allan shouted. "On your right!"

Robert turned and saw a confused-looking guard with a purple face moving toward them, his gait awkward, uneven.

He stepped toward the man and held out his hand, concentrating as he had before. At first, nothing happened—the man continued to move toward them. But a second later, the man's eyebrows furrowed, and he slowed. A few seconds after that, he came to a complete stop.

"Another! Behind him!" Allan shouted.

Robert looked over the first guard, and caught sight of another quiddity, this one walking in a small, tight circle. He was muttering something to himself, but with the sound of the Marrow rushing in his ears, Robert couldn't make out the words.

Moving his hand slightly higher, the man's circles slowed and then he too stopped completely.

There was a grunt from his left, but when he looked over, the only thing he saw was a swinging corpse.

"Human!" Sean shouted.

A burst of gunfire erupted and the corpse that was within three feet of Robert exploded like a bag of red paint. Through the gaping wound in the man's torso, he caught sight of a man in a white t-shirt stumbling backward. Another burst of gunfire through the hole, and the man disappeared in his own personal shower of red and white.

Shelly screamed, and he heard Cal cry out.

"Bogey!" Sean yelled.

Robert lifted his gaze in time to see another man rushing toward him. Sean's pistol cracked off three tight rounds, and two red dots formed on his white t-shirt. The third bullet hit him square in the forehead, and his eyes rolled back before he fell face first onto the ground.

Robert's chest had gotten so tight that it was getting hard to draw even a partial breath. Still with his hand out, he moved forward even farther, cutting the distance to the door on the other end of the mess hall by a third.

But then he saw them. Six or seven lost, confused souls coming at him, blocking his way.

"Stop!" he shouted, raising his other hand. A terrible crushing sensation nearly crippled him, but the quiddity obeyed. Robert took an agonizing step forward. And then another.

"Robert!"

He ignored the shout.

Must keep moving…

He was holding at least eight quiddity at bay now, and he had nearly made it to the far door.

"Look out!" Shelly cried, but Robert, concentrating as he was, turned too slowly.

One of the hanging corpses was suddenly thrust into him, knocking him to the ground.

"Fuck!" he yelled, his elbows taking most of the impact.

He tried to scramble to his feet, but something struck him hard in the back, forcing him down again.

"You'll never get to him," someone whispered in his ear, the breath hot and sweet. A hand grabbed the back of his hair, pulling his head up. "Carson sends his regards."

"Help!" he gasped, fearing that his face was about to be smashed on the hard ground. But just as he felt the grip in his hair tighten, he heard another scream and the fingers let go.

Robert quickly spun and scooted out of the way, peering up at his assailant.

The man had a narrow face with short, well-groomed hair. He looked more like an accountant—like Robert—than a murderer. But the look in his eyes...

Robert pushed himself backward, watching as the man's eyes started to cloud.

And then he saw the guard, Quinn, behind the inmate, wrapping his arms around him. He looked frightened, which was saying something, given the fact that he had no eyes.

Thank you, Robert mouthed, not knowing if on some level the man *could* see.

He thought he saw the man nod before the inmate threw his head back in a howl and then the two of them started to fade.

Gunfire erupted from somewhere behind him—first Aiden's weapon, then the distinct *bap bap bap* of Sean's pistol. He wanted to go to his friends, to Shelly, to see if they were safe, but he couldn't. He had to get to the rift.

That was his only goal now.

Cal had been right. This was bigger than him, than all of them.

Robert pulled himself onto his haunches and then tried to stand. Still feeling the pain from the tackle, he staggered, but eventually managed to maintain his balance.

The door was only a dozen feet from him, if that.

Almost there...

But then two inmates stepped out from behind hanging corpses, blocking his path.

"You won't get to him," they sneered in unison.

Robert's heart sank.

"Sean! Aiden!" he cried over his shoulder, but considering the chaos and gunfire, it seemed unlikely that they would have heard him.

The two men, one with his shirt off, revealing a series of blue and red tattoos that crisscrossed his muscular chest, the other with a scar that ran across his forehead and receded into the dark stubble on the top of his skull, stepped toward Robert.

This is it…I've failed.

"I'm sorry, Amy," he said.

It wasn't like him to concede, but there was nothing he could do. He wasn't a fighter, and ordering these men to stop would accomplish nothing.

The man on the left, with the scar on his head, laughed.

"She's comin'…she's comin' to set us all free."

Just as Robert gave up hope, the door behind the two inmates swung open. Another man, a small, thin man with his hands tucked behind his back, half lunged, half tumbled into the shirtless inmate. The movement was so awkward that he actually managed to take the much larger man down with him.

"Fuck!" the other inmate shouted.

Uninspired last words, as they were.

His left side just above the hip bone exploded, and Robert's hands immediately went to his ears. Another blast rang out and the man stared down at himself, confused as to what had happened.

The second shotgun blast cut him clean in half, soaking Robert in his blood and viscera and bits of bone.

A man stood in the doorway, a smoking shotgun in his hand, another wrapped across his chest. He was bald and looked in his mid-sixties, with the thick, muscular forearms of a much younger man.

Robert blinked, trying to figure out what the fuck had just happened. Then he noticed the navy uniform that matched those that hung all around them.

One guard must have gotten away.

Robert's relief was short-lived; the other inmate recovered from his fall.

"Get the fuck off me," he said, shoving the other man off of him. Only now did Robert realize that the man's hands were bound behind his back.

The guard with the shotgun turned his attention to the other inmate as the latter scrambled to his feet. But before he could open fire, Sean stepped out from behind a body and shot the inmate directly in the head, sending him falling back down again. He moved the gun to the other man, the one with his hands tied behind him, next.

"No!" Robert and the guard with the shotgun yelled in unison, but they were too late.

Sean shot him in the head, too.

Robert stepped forward, his mouth hanging open in horror.

"Sean! Sean, why the hell did—"

Sean Sommer's eyes whipped up.

"He was gone, Robert. He was gone! Didn't you see his eyes? Leland got to him…and when that man touches you, the poison spreads fast."

Robert glanced down at the dead man with his hands tied behind his back. His eyes were vacant as they stared lifelessly at the ceiling.

Then Sean turned toward them, the all too familiar tight-lipped expression returning to his face.

"He was gone!" he shouted suddenly. "Go to Carson before it's too late! Go! *Go!*"

Chapter 41

ROBERT, FACE AND ARMS covered in blood and organ meat, veritably threw himself over the threshold of Carson's cell.

And then he immediately backpedaled. He probably would have gone right out the door if not for the fact that the man in the guard uniform and Sean were standing behind him.

"Fuck," Robert said breathlessly.

The man named Carson was sitting on the floor, his back to the door, as was a woman whom he had never seen before. In the middle, however, was what was left of Father Callahan.

His body had been split down the middle, and he was lying with his arms spread, each of his hands grasped in the laps of the two seated individuals.

Intestines spilled out on either side of the man's torn torso, but it was what was in between that took Robert's breath away. Instead of blood-covered floor, Robert was staring *into* the floor, through it, and into the Marrow. As he gaped at the Marrow, he could make out the burning sky and a figure on the beach.

One that looked familiar.

One with a large black hat and a faded jean jacket.

"No!" he yelled.

His shout drew the attention of Carson, who craned his head around to look at Robert.

Again, Robert tried to move backward, but the burly guard caught him and made sure he didn't fall.

The man on the floor was thinner, with a narrower nose and wider set eyes, but there was no doubting it.

He looked like Robert.

"Oh, hey, brother. Long time no see. How you been, anyway?"

And then he laughed.

Robert blinked hard, unable to understand what he was seeing.

Brother? This is my brother?

Noticing the confusion in his eyes, Carson's lifted his gaze to Sean behind Robert.

"You didn't tell him?"

Robert whipped his head around to stare at Sean, whose eyes were locked on Carson.

"Oh, okay. Well then, Robert, did Sean tell you that daddy's coming?"

Robert glanced back to the hole in Father Callahan's chest. It appeared that the man was getting closer, somehow crawling *upward.*

"What the fuck is going on?" Robert yelled, grabbing at his hair.

He felt a nudge on his back, and turned in time to see Sean handing him the pistol. For some reason, he took it, and then immediately leveled it Carson's head.

"Tell me what's going on or I'll blow your head off."

Carson just stared at him, a confused expression on his face. Then his face broke into a grin.

"Sean? Do you want to do the honors?"

"Shoot him," Sean responded simply. "Close the rift before it's too late."

Robert whipped his head and the gun around to Sean. Then he turned back again to Carson.

"Suit yourself. But now that we are in the mood for a little storytelling, did Sean tell you what he did? Hmm? What he and this so-called 'priest' did?"

Robert looked to the man splayed out on the ground, hot white light spilling from his eyes and face.

"Shoot him," Sean repeated.

"Shut up!" Robert shouted back.

"Yeah, that prick that you've been following around like a lost puppy? And this priest that you're here to save? Well they hunted once too. They hunted down our father, Robert— hunted him down and killed him. But Sean didn't tell you that, did he?"

Robert's brow narrowed.

"What's he talking about?"

"Ignore him and pull the trigger, Robert."

"Fine, listen to Sean. Shoot me, I don't care. It won't close the gate now, Robert."

"What's he talking about?" Robert asked again, the gun in his hand wavering slightly. "Did you kill Leland, Sean?"

"Robert..."

Robert whipped around, and took a step away from Sean. He pointed the gun at his chest. The man's expression didn't change.

"Is it true?"

Sean pursed his lips defiantly.

"Fucking answer me!" Robert demanded. "I'm sick of your fucking games, Sean. Answer me or I swear to—"

"Yes," he said simply. "Yes, we killed him."

He offered no reasoning. He said it just like a Jeopardy answer.

Yes, we killed him.

"Fuck!" Robert squeezed his eyes tight and gritted his teeth. The hand not holding the gun went to his hair and he pulled once more. Then his legs gave way and he collapsed to the ground.

"Come with me, Robert," he heard Carson say over the roaring waves. "Come with me and be reunited with our father."

"No," Robert whispered, shaking his head back and forth. "I can't—I don't—I—"

Then someone else in the room finally spoke up.

"Best I shoot him, then." The man's voice was hoarse as if he too had been crying not so long ago. "I don't know what the fuck you did to Father Callahan, but you're gonna pay."

Robert opened his eyes and stared at the large, bald guard.

"We can't shoot him...if we kill Carson like this, the rift will stay open forever."

Carson laughed.

"Oh, so you got the brains of the two of us, Robert. That's good. We can use your brains."

"Fuck this," Ben said, stepping forward. "I'm—"

"No," Sean said softly. "He's right. Killing Carson will keep the door open. The only way to close the rift now is to—"

"—to kill the priest," Robert said quietly. He slowly rose to his feet and moved the gun sight from Carson to Father Callahan's glowing head.

For the first time since entering the room, the smile slid off Carson's face.

"Don't do it," Robert's brother growled. "Don't even think about it."

Robert ignored Carson and stared into the priest's chest cavity. Leland was close now, he was right near the surface.

Tears filled his eyes with the realization of what he had to do.

But before he could act, the warden of Seaforth Prison spoke again.

"Now that *definitely* ain't happening."

Robert turned around and was shocked to see that Ben had his shotgun out again, but this time it was aimed at his chest.

"I don't know what the fuck is going on here, but I've been through a lot of shit today, and it all boils down to this: I'm not letting you kill this man...my friend, Father Callahan. No way, no how."

Chapter 42

CAL GODFREY DIDN'T DARE move. At some point during the melee, someone had fallen on him—he didn't know if it was one of the hanged guards or an inmate that had been blown away by Aiden's assault rifle—and while he tried to get up, to wipe the blood from his face and rise, another had fallen on him.

Before he knew it, three or four more or less complete bodies had piled on top of him and he couldn't for the life of him get up. So he did the next best thing.

He lay there, cowering in his dank, foul-smelling pile of corpses, and waited.

For nearly six minutes, he lay completely still, listening to the sound of gunfire and shouts from somewhere high above him. And then, out of nowhere, it stopped completely.

Cal's breathing was shallow, partly because he wanted to remain hidden, and partly because he was trying to avoid breathing in too much of the blood and other fluids that seemed to cover his entire body. He felt shame, shame for being such a coward at leaving Allan and Shelly with Aiden.

The man seemed capable, surely, much more so than Cal himself, but *he* had brought Allan here. He was the one who had acquiesced to Sean's request to come to Seaforth Prison. The man had said that they were needed, required, to purge the quiddity, and yet he had simply left them there to die.

Or worse.

Cal shook his head.

At the time, the strangeness of Sean coming to him, especially given the fact that all previous encounters had only been with Robert, had dawned on him. But his pride had forced him to gloss over that fact.

But now, cowering as he was, he understood.

Cal hadn't been recruited to purge any ghosts, not in the least.

Sean had asked him to come here just in case Robert refused the offer. Cal and Allan were bait.

"Get up," a muffled voice instructed.

Cal, uncertain who was speaking, and who the person was speaking to, froze.

"Up," the voice repeated.

Cal still didn't move.

A sliver of the dull gray light suddenly hit him in the eye as one of the corpses was peeled off. He squinted as another body was tossed aside and the intensity of the light increased.

Then a familiar face peeked in, a wad of dip still tucked into his lower lip.

"We gotta go," Aiden said, leaning in with his hand.

Cal stared at it for a second.

"Is it over?"

The man shook his head.

"Nope. More coming, we need to move now."

Cal reached out and grabbed the man's hand. His grip was tight, unforgiving. Then, with one yank, Cal found himself on his feet again.

His t-shirt and jeans clung to him uncomfortably, and it was all he could do to not look down at the gore that he knew he was soaked with. He blinked several times, but the sensation was strange as his lids were tacky with blood and kept sticking together.

He looked around and cringed at the carnage.

There were bodies everywhere, hanging, lying on the ground, even stuck to the walls.

"Fuuuuuck," he moaned, unable to help himself.

"Fuck is right," a female voice to his left said sharply. "You done hiding?"

Cal turned to stare at Shelly, who looked as horrible as he felt. Her hair, usually platinum blonde, was completely red, and blood streaked her cheeks.

"You look like shit," she said, pressing her lips together.

"You too," he replied.

"Let's go. Don't know how many more of them there are," Aiden said, "but they're coming.

Cal looked around Shelly, searching for Allan.

He found him standing by the entrance to the mess hall, looking like he had aged more than a decade over the past hour. One of the lenses of his glasses was smashed, and the camera he held in his hand had been reduced to a hunk of metal and plastic. Cal even thought he could see a bullet embedded in case, and yet the boy still held it as if he were going to take some Pulitzer-worthy photos.

Glancing around, Cal was glad that the camera was broken. There was no need to have visual proof of what happened here, a reminder of the horror.

Best if this was all forgotten. If that was at all possible.

"Wait—where's Robert?" he asked suddenly.

Aiden just shook his head. For all of the gore that covered Cal, Shelly, and Allen, Aiden was relatively clean. Aside from some blood on his boots, the lower half of his pants and the muzzle of his assault rifle, he looked much like he had when Cal had first seen him in the hallway less than an hour ago.

"Wait, wait, wait," Cal said quickly. "No way. I'm not leaving without Robbo."

Aiden shook his head again and raised his gun. Cal didn't perceive this as an aggressive gesture, more like a simple reminder.

"Sean gave specific instructions. We need to leave, *now!*"

He took a step forward, and Cal was surprised that Shelly actually moved toward the door with him.

"I'm not leaving—"

"Oh, so now you are mister bravery? Is that it?" Shelly demanded, her expression transitioning into a scowl. "A few minutes ago, you were—"

The static of a radio interrupted her.

"Mark, bring the chopper in. Get the gray ready."

Cal eyed him.

The gray? What the fuck is the gray?

Aiden didn't wait for a response. Instead, he clicked the walkie to his belt and then motioned to the door with the muzzle of his gun.

"Move. Now."

Shelly hurried toward the door, making it to Allan's side, but Cal refused and held his ground.

"I won't—"

"Move, or I'll knock you out and drag your body out the door."

For good measure, he spat a wad of brown juice onto the floor at Cal's feet.

What choice did he have?

Cal reluctantly turned and hurried after Shelly and Allan.

When he got to the door, he made a final turn, his stomach twisting into a knot as he surveyed the carnage once more.

I'm sorry, Robert. I'm so, so sorry.

And then the four of them left Seaforth Prison.

Chapter 43

"YOU SHOOT FATHER CALLAHAN, and I'll cut you in half," Ben informed him.

Robert's eyes whipped back and forth, jumping from Ben to Sean to Carson to Father Callahan's ruined body.

"He's gone," Sean said. "We need to close the rift."

Movement in the center of the priest's chest drew Robert's gaze.

Fingers appeared, grasping the sides of Callahan's ribcage, pushing into the man's innards. They tensed, as if preparing to hoist something out.

Someone out.

It was Leland.

"Hurry, Robert, close the rift!" Sean shouted.

"Ohhhhh, Daddy's here!" Carson said gleefully. "Wait for Daddy, Rrrrrrobbo!"

Robert's finger tensed on the trigger.

"I'm warning you," Ben said calmly.

Robert stared at the hands protruding from Father Callahan's body cavity, and then his heart skipped a beat when the top of a black hat appeared.

Whatever he decided, he had to do it soon; otherwise his decision would be for naught.

The light suddenly blinked out of Father Callahan's eyes and mouth, and the man somehow managed to move his neck. His eye holes were smoking, the eyes themselves long since melted away by whatever energy had made him a conduit. His mouth was likewise a blackened, molten mess.

"Father!" Ben shouted.

Despite the words coming from Robert's right, the priest's head turned toward him. And then the lips started to move, silently forming words.

Close the rift, Robert. And then get the book. Get Inter vivos et mortuos.

Robert wasn't sure if he was lip reading, or if the words were actually in his head.

"Father!" Ben shouted again, then he made the mistake of lowering the gun and sliding closer to the fallen man.

Sean acted quickly and decisively. His left arm shot out and swatted the shotgun to one side before the older man could react. Ben cried out and tried to regain control, but Sean grabbed his arm next, and pulled him forward, fueling his momentum.

Inter vivos et mortuos.

The priest mouthed over and over and over again.

Inter vivos et mortuos.

Robert's eyes flicked from Carson, who was beaming, to Father Callahan's horribly mangled mouth.

Do it. Close the rift. Please.

Back and forth Robert's eyes bounced.

And then another voice entered the fray.

It was the Goat.

"Robert? That you again, Robert? Oh, how I've—"

Robert closed his eyes and fired a single shot.

Someone screamed, but Robert had no idea who. The vibrations from Sean's gun were surprisingly powerful, and it fell from his hand.

"No! Robert! No!"

Robert opened his eyes and stared directly into the horrible face that was peeking out of the Marrow, everything but the eyes visible from beneath the large brim of the black hat.

Only it wasn't a skull or a demon like he had expected, that he tried desperately but couldn't remember from the first time he had met Leland, his father.

Instead, Robert was staring into *his* face. Older, more weathered, but undeniably *his* face.

And then the man's mouth opened in a scream, and he fell back, his hands flailing as he cascaded into the sea below.

"You motherfucker!" Ben screamed.

Robert turned just in time to see the Warden regain his balance and aim the shotgun at him. Robert didn't move, didn't even try to avoid the blast. Instead, he accepted what was coming, the image of Father Callahan's slack face, a smoldering bullet hole in his forehead etched in his mind.

But the blast he expected never came, and Robert eventually opened his eyes again.

Sean had somehow managed to trip Ben, and the man stumbled. When his foot hit Father Callahan's lifeless leg, he slipped.

And then he too went tumbling into the narrowing hole in the priest's chest to the Marrow Sea below.

Carson jumped to his feet, screaming in anger. His face twisted into a horrible sneer.

"Robert! What have you done?"

Robert, fighting back tears, raised the gun at the brother that two days ago he'd never known he had.

"Go," he said over his shoulder to Sean. "Get the fuck out of here before I shoot you, too."

When the man didn't move, Robert started to scream.

"Get the fuck out of here!"

Sean bolted for the door, pulling it wide and sprinting from the room.

Finally, Robert turned back to his brother, the gun still aimed at the man's thin, naked chest.

Carson spat on the floor at their feet.

"What, now you're going to shoot your brother in cold blood?"

Robert clenched his teeth.

"You know, we're not so different, are we?"

And then the smile returned to Carson's face.

EPILOGUE

AIDEN SET THE FINAL charge at the base of the front door to Seaforth Prison, before turning back to the helicopter. The wind and rain was still relentless, but it didn't bother him as much as the others.

He had been through worse—much worse.

Pressing the radio receiver into the gray, briefcase-sized block of C4, he started to walk backwards toward the helicopter, all the while keeping his rifle aimed at the door.

He had his orders.

They were to leave, with or without Sean and Robert. They had to get the package to safety.

There was still one Guardian left, and they needed to keep it that way.

Static erupted from the walkie on his belt.

It was Mark.

"Ready to lift, Aiden. Get your ass in here."

Aiden nodded, not sure if his friend could see him through the rain, but not caring either way.

When the sound of the helicopter blades became loud enough to block out the rain, he turned and sprinted the rest of the way to the chopper. He could see three faces inside, three pale, scared civilians that had no reason to be here.

He was barely inside when the man named Cal started shouting at him.

"Are those explosives? Are you going to blow up the prison?" His voice was shrill, his eyes wide.

Aiden didn't answer. Instead, he put an index finger in the air and spun it in a circle. Mark, peering back at him from the cockpit, nodded, then turned his attention to the controls.

"It is, isn't it? We can't—Robert—we—"

Shelly started on him next.

"We can't fucking leave him here! He's still inside! You have to wait!"

Aiden couldn't help but feel a pang of guilt looking at her pretty face, contorted the way it was.

She loved him, Aiden knew. He knew, because he had seen the same look on his wife's face when she had still been alive.

He cleared his throat.

"Take us up, Mark."

"No!" Shelly shouted. She reached for him, and he quickly moved the gun to the other side, out of her reach. Her fists rained down on his arm, but Aiden kept his eyes trained straight ahead.

A second later, he felt the familiar lurch in his stomach as the helicopter slowly started to rise off the ground.

"No! Please! You can't do this!" Shelly pleaded. Cal started to reach for him too, but he shoved the man away with a strong hand.

"Wait!" This time it was Mark, and Aiden raised his head. "There! Someone's coming out, stay hot, Aiden."

Aiden shifted so that he was by the open helicopter door, and raised his gun again, his finger on the trigger.

A second later, he lifted his finger.

It was Sean Sommers.

"Bring 'er down again, Mark!"

The helicopter lowered again.

"Is it him?! Shel, is it *him?*"

Even the kid, who had been silent for so long now that Aiden feared for his sanity, leaned forward and spoke.

"Is it Robert?"

Shelly tried to push by Aiden to get a better look, but he shifted his body so that she wouldn't be tempted to jump out.

"It's—I dunno—"

"Hurry!" Aiden shouted, waving his free arm frantically.

"Fuck! It's not him! Cal, it's not him!"

"No!"

Sean ran to the helicopter, the rain and wind pelting him, serving to wash off some of the grime that covered his previously white shirt and blond hair.

Aiden helped hoist the man into the helicopter, who promptly collapsed into the nearest seat, his eyes closed, his head hung low.

"Mark, get us out of here...I'm gonna blow this place."

This time, there was no response from either Cal or Shelly.

"Aiden?" Mark said.

"Yeah?"

"There's one more...there's someone else coming out of the prison."

***

Carson Ford sprinted from his cell and burst into the hallway.

He couldn't believe that he had failed, that Robert of all people had fucked things up. All of the years of preparation were lost because he had underestimated his own kin.

But Leland had been smart. Leland had made sure that he had an escape plan, despite Carson insisting that it wasn't necessary.

Lungs burning, knowing that he had little time, Carson pumped his arms and legs, tearing through Cell Block E, the place that he had called home for nearly a decade. He knew where he was headed.

Carson burst through the door to the chapel, and ran through the aisle without hesitation. He rammed his hands into the altar at full speed, ignoring the pain in his wrists as he shoved the solid piece of marble toward the back wall.

His blood pumped in his ears, and his vision narrowed.

The altar butted against the back wall, driving more pain into his wrists that also went ignored. In one fluid movement, he hoisted himself onto the makeshift table, and then scrabbled more than three feet up the bricks before throwing his body through the stained-glass window depicting Jesus on the cross.

The pain from the cuts all over his body was quickly replaced by the stinging sensation of the freezing rain and wind.

Carson landed on the top of the dumpster that he had convinced Peter to put there for him. The initial drop was more than ten feet, and he jammed his right ankle on landing despite rolling with the fall. The injury caused him to tilt to one side, and his back smashed into the corner of a cement step more than six feet below. The air was forced out of his lungs and he saw stars. For a second, he did nothing; he just stared up at the rain, trying desperately to catch his breath.

Somewhere in the distance, he heard the sound of helicopter blades chuffing, and he grunted and rolled onto his front. A moment later, he was up and running again.

Carson didn't hesitate when he hit the shore. He dove head first.

As he pumped his legs and blew air from his nose in the icy cold water, the sky above him erupted into a fantastic ball of fire. The ocean suddenly became turbulent, clawing at his hands and feet like tiny hands, the undertow from the collapsing Seaforth Prison threatening to make this his final resting place.

But Carson kicked hard, and concentrated on holding his breath for as long as possible.

Years of training in his cell came in handy, as he'd known it would.

Forty yards from the collapsing inferno, the dark outline of a head poked out of the water. The head bobbed for a moment, and then it plunged back into the depths below.

END

Author's Note

For a long while now, I have been fascinated with the idea of self-awareness. Artificial intelligence, universal morality, and—in Sam Harris' words—understanding what it means to be *something*, if it means anything at all, are topics that I expend considerable energy exploring. And for whatever reason, Carl Jung's psychological philosophies have stuck with me since I was first introduced to his ideas decades ago. As a forever pragmatist, I'm not sure that I believe much, or any of his writings, but what should be obvious after reading Seaforth Prison is that in the very least I find them captivating and worthy of contemplation.

I hope you enjoyed Seaforth Prison. There is more of this tale to tell…there are many more mysteries to unravel in this world. You can find Book 4 of the Haunted Series, *SCARSDALE CREMATORIUM* on pre-order now. So point your browser to Amazon if you want to continue joining Rob, Shelly, and Cal on their adventures.

Leland knows, they'd be lonely without you.

Keep on reading and I'll keep on writing,
Patrick
Montreal, 2016

CPSIA information can be obtained
at www.ICGtesting.com
Printed in the USA
LVOW12s1833060717
540469LV00005B/890/P